SAVE ME

(A Katie Winter FBI Suspense Thriller —Book 1)

Molly Black

Molly Black

Debut author Molly Black is author of the MAYA GRAY FBI suspense thriller series, comprising six books (and counting); the RYLIE WOLF FBI suspense thriller series, comprising three books (and counting); of the TAYLOR SAGE FBI suspense thriller series, comprising three books (and counting); and of the KATIE WINTER FBI suspense thriller series, comprising three books (and counting).

An avid reader and lifelong fan of the mystery and thriller genres, Molly loves to hear from you, so please feel free to visit www.mollyblackauthor.com to learn more and stay in touch.

ISBN: 978-1-0943-9400-8

BOOKS BY MOLLY BLACK

MAYA GRAY MYSTERY SERIES
GIRL ONE: MURDER (Book #1)
GIRL TWO: TAKEN (Book #2)
GIRL THREE: TRAPPED (Book #3)
GIRL FOUR: LURED (Book #4)
GIRL FIVE: BOUND (Book #5)
GIRL SIX: FORSAKEN (Book #6)

RYLIE WOLF FBI SUSPENSE THRILLER
FOUND YOU (Book #1)
CAUGHT YOU (Book #2)
SEE YOU (Book #3)

TAYLOR SAGE FBI SUSPENSE THRILLER
DON'T LOOK (Book #1)
DON'T BREATHE (Book #2)
DON'T RUN (Book #3)

KATIE WINTER FBI SUSPENSE THRILLER
SAVE ME (Book #1)
REACH ME (Book #2)
HIDE ME (Book #3)

CHAPTER ONE

The gray-haired man scrambled to his feet, his knees protesting his 60 years, staring curiously at the object fluttering across the lake's frozen surface.

He squinted, struggling to focus so that he could determine what it was. But the breeze tugged it in the other direction, sending it skittering away across the ice as he tried to comprehend what he was seeing.

Was it a bracelet? Or something else?

Yesterday he'd picked up a fishing lure that had fallen off during one of his previous attempts. Finding the lure had encouraged him to continue, to brave the cold a little longer.

Today was not going well. He had been having a bad streak, and he had a feeling it was about to get worse. So far, the only thing he had to show for his efforts was a purple lump on his forehead from where he'd slipped on the ice. And the wind was picking up.

Perhaps he should go back to his cabin, he thought, and try again tomorrow. He returned his attention to his fishing pole, but then, glancing up, he saw it again, this time a little closer.

"What could it be?" he whispered to himself.

It was small and every time the wind blew, it would move a couple of feet. Treading carefully over the ice, he made his way closer.

When he bent to pick it up, he saw it was a glimmering, sequined hair tie. A scrunchie, as his granddaughter called them.

His heart pounded as he saw this one was covered in blood.

He stared around in concern. This object must have come from somewhere. But where?

As he surveyed the lake again, this time, he saw it, camouflaged by a drift of snow. A crack in the ice.

No, not a crack. This dark shape looked like something different. Was it a rock?

He forced his legs to move, stumbling closer. As he neared it, he started to fear the worst. This didn't look like a rock.

He gasped as he realized what he was seeing, trapped in a solidifying layer of ice.

It was a body.

A woman.

Frozen in the water, her matted blonde hair partially covering her face. Her eyes were wide open, and in horror, he realized the ice had frozen them in place.

"No," he whispered.

Shaking with the effort and cold, he leaned carefully forward and touched her outstretched arm. Her body was stiff and unresponsive.

He reached into his pocket, groping for his phone to call 911.

But he fumbled, and his phone slipped out of his trembling hands and smashed down onto the ice, its screen cracking.

The man stood there, utterly alone with her, feeling as helpless as he had ever been, just he and this woman, alone out here.

Sinking to his knees, he wept.

CHAPTER TWO

FBI Special Agent Katie Winter stood outside the shack, gun drawn, and checked her ammunition for the third time. She released the safety, took a deep breath, closed her eyes, and prepared for the worst.

There was a killer behind those doors, ready to take her life as soon as she would take his. A seasoned criminal, he'd broken out of the prison van on the way to the courthouse in Norfolk, Virginia, yesterday. He'd killed a guard and gone on the run. Now, he was holed up in here, armed and dangerous.

All around her, the SWAT team swarmed, ready for the dawn raid. Tension and focus sizzled in the air as she heard their murmured voices. She knew she had backup.

But that did not put her at ease. Relying on others was a sure way to get killed. She had seen it happen too many times. And this was her case. She would take the lead.

At five- foot-eight, with dark brown hair pulled back in a bun, and feeling much older than her 32 years, Katie was as good of a shot as all these SWAT men. She had taken down more killers than she wanted to remember in her ten years with the FBI. But each one brought something new and unpredictable.

She remembered the first case she worked. It was a routine affair, a simple bank robbery that went terribly wrong. She was the only one of her team to make it out alive.

She closed her eyes and tried to shake the image from her mind, but her thoughts became jumbled. She felt nauseous and the sounds around her mingled with the memories of gunshots and screams.

Breathing deeply, she suppressed the memories, forcing herself to stay focused.

She readied herself. Three… two… one…

"Go!" she yelled.

She kicked the door open with a mighty bang. It flew off the hinges, crashing to the side onto the dirt floor. Holding her breath, she ran inside, gun at the ready as she led the way.

It all happened in a blur.

There he was. And as the cold morning light streamed into the dusty, tumbledown building, Katie saw he was not alone.

He had someone with him. He had taken a hostage.

Katie had been prepared to meet the killer and stop him in his tracks. But now she knew there was more at stake than just her own safety.

The fear for another innocent life clenched her stomach. She hadn't expected a hostage situation.

"Wait! Stay back!" she shouted to the team.

She stared at the man. Wiry, in his late twenties, with a shaved head and an athletic frame, he wore a black leather jacket and had a few days of scruff on his face. He had his gun jammed into the woman's temple.

Cowering and confused, the hostage was crying in terror. Her sobs only seemed to enrage him more.

"Drop your weapon!" Katie shouted. "Drop it now!"

"I don't think so, lady," the killer sneered. He smiled, and Katie saw blood staining his chin and neck. Whose blood, she wondered. Had he been wounded during the chase? Or was it the hostage's?

"She got nothing to live for anyway."

The words chilled her. His voice was deep and coarse. And the way he looked at the hostage, Katie knew he was going to kill her.

"Drop it!"

"Make me."

Aiming carefully, Katie had him in her sights, ready to take the shot. If she could get a clean head shot, she could drop him before he could shoot the sobbing woman.

But, at that moment, a rookie SWAT agent burst in behind her and spooked him.

Jerking his gun in the direction of his attackers, the killer fired three times. The shots exploded around her. Katie hit the floor, rolling, as the SWAT agent went down.

This was turning into a disaster. Dust billowed from the filthy floor, choking her, blinding her. She struggled into a kneeling position, blinking tears from her eyes, expecting at any moment to feel his bullet punch into her.

But, as the dust cleared, she saw to her astonishment that he had gone. And the hostage, too. He'd taken her with him.

She couldn't believe it. It was like he vanished.

Then she saw the open hole in the floor.

A trapdoor.

In a rush, the other three members of the SWAT team entered the shack.

"Quick, call a medic. This guy's hurt," the lead agent yelled. "You okay?" he asked Katie, his voice urgent.

"I'm fine. But he's taken the hostage," Katie could hear the tension thrumming in her own voice.

"This door must lead down to a cellar."

Snapping on a flashlight, the lead agent shone it into the trapdoor, revealing a steep wooden staircase. He scrambled down, followed by the others.

Katie was about to follow. But then she thought again. She knew this killer. He was a master of misdirection, sneaky and slippery.

The backyard, she realized. The trapdoor might be a decoy. He wouldn't let himself be cornered down there. He would find a way to escape.

She had to stop him.

Gun in hand, ready to fire, she crept toward the shack's back door. She guessed he wasn't going to run blindly. Not with a SWAT team in pursuit. Instead, he would choose to double back, burst in and try to destroy the threat before escaping.

Were her instincts correct?

Hearing a breath of noise outside, she pushed it open, and gasped as she found herself face-to-face with the killer.

Holding the hostage, the woman's arm cruelly twisted up behind her back, he was pointing his gun right at her.

She dropped to her knees, unable to risk firing on the hostage, just as he shot at her. The noise exploded in her ears. He must have missed by only an inch.

But, as she dropped, she saw her chance and fired at his outstretched arm, winging his elbow. Screaming, he dropped the woman. He turned and fled.

"He's released her. Get her to safety!" Katie shouted to her team. "He's run outside."

She couldn't let him get away again. She jumped up and sprinted in pursuit.

He stormed through the neglected backyard and into the thick weeds and thorns of the wild forest.

The chase was on.

The thought of losing him--or someone getting killed--was all that drove her.

The early rays of the sun were just peeking over the trees, lighting the way in front of her, but he was ahead, and he clearly knew the area better than she did. As she crashed behind, fighting through the undergrowth, she realized she had lost him in the thick vegetation. She guessed this area must be familiar terrain to him. He knew how to navigate through it. How to hide and how to circle back. He'd done it once. It was his modus operandi and he might do it again.

She paused, listening for any sound, standing as still as she could on the loose, shifting dirt and stones of the forest floor.

There was no birdsong, no rustling of leaves, nothing. The silence was unnerving.

Around her, the forest was dense and impenetrable, a place of dark shadows, sudden turns, and hidden danger.

She didn't hear the killer in the woods behind her.

She didn't hear any sound of footsteps or the swishing of his clothing. She didn't hear the sound of his breathing.

But she did hear something, sharp and frightening.

A snap of a twig behind her that made her jump.

And then, shockingly, his voice rang out, sharp and authoritative.

"Don't turn around. My gun is aimed at your head, and I'll shoot if you move. Drop your weapon. Now."

Katie's heart raced. By circling back through the forest he knew so well, he'd effectively trapped her.

Her nightmares surged inside her. She knew she should try to shoot. But she couldn't. If she lifted her weapon, she would die.

She let go of the gun and it fell to the ground.

At any moment she expected to feel the deadly punch of a bullet in the back. Or maybe he would go for a head shot and she would feel nothing at all. There would just be a burst of darkness and it would all be over.

"Move away," he whispered. "Move back."

Slowly, she backed three strides away, her shoes scrunching over stones.

"Now you can turn," he ordered.

With her hands raised, she slowly turned.

He was standing in the path a few paces away, smiling. The expression was utterly evil. He was reveling in his power.

She knew his mindset from the research she'd done. He liked to kill up close and personal. To see the fear in his victims' eyes before he pulled the trigger.

He took another step toward her.

She wasn't going to let him win, but she had only a few moments left before she lost.

He was a few feet from her now, and she had to do something to distract him before he fired.

She inhaled deeply, making herself think, forcing herself to overcome the fear and to focus.

There was one thing he would never expect.

With a shout, she kicked into the dirt as hard as she could, sending up a spray of sand and stones. Instinctively, he flinched away, turning his head to protect his eyes. His gun swung wide.

Seizing the moment, leaping forward, she attacked. With all the strength she could muster, she smashed her fists into his face.

The killer staggered backward, stumbling over a tree root. Blood poured from his nose and mouth.

"You bitch," he snarled.

He raised his gun. She dove to the side.

He fired and the bullet whistled past her head as she lunged for his arm. Her hand smashed into his elbow, punching into the place where her bullet had winged him earlier.

He shrieked in agony. The gun flew out of his hand and skidded across the stony soil. Lifting her knee, she jabbed it into his stomach, knocking the wind out of him.

He gasped, rolled onto his side, fighting for breath. She dove at him and slammed her knee into his gut once more.

He crumpled with a cry of agony.

Katie's hand closed around the back of his neck. She yanked his head back and brought her knee up into his face, smashing his nose.

Finally, he went limp.

She dropped him and he hit the dirt. The stony ground bit into her knees as she cuffed him.

She grabbed his gun, and retrieved her own weapon.

Then she reached for her phone and called the SWAT operatives.

“I’ve got him,” she said, sending her coordinates.

This had been a dangerous operation and it hadn’t gone according to plan. One of her team had been shot and injured; she still didn’t know how badly. She didn’t know if the hostage was hurt. Would her bosses think she’d handled it correctly?

As these worries raced through her mind, Katie's phone buzzed. Grabbing it, she saw it was a text from her immediate boss, FBI Senior Special Agent Andrews.

"Winter, I need to see you urgently. Meet me in the office as soon as you can."

CHAPTER THREE

Arriving at the FBI office in Chesapeake, Virginia, that afternoon, Katie rushed inside, concerned. Why did Andrews need to see her so urgently?

She replayed the takedown again and again in her mind, wishing she could have predicted all the twists it had taken. With a degree in criminal psychology and experience in chasing down serial killers, she knew she was expected to think on her feet and stay one step ahead. Had she done enough?

As soon as she hurried out of the elevator, onto the third floor of the large glass-and concrete-clad building, she saw Andrews, her boss, waiting.

The lean man, with his hair graying at the temples, looked satisfied.

"Katie, fine work this morning."

She felt relief wash over her.

"Thanks," she said, not letting him see how worried she'd been.

"I've already met with the prosecutor. He said they'll be seeking the harshest sentence. No bail, of course. Since he's escaped from prison before, they're taking no chances and he'll go straight into a maximum security cell."

"Is he cooperating with police?" she asked.

"Not yet. "

"What about the hostage, and the injured SWAT team member?" Katie asked.

"She's already back with her family and will be receiving counseling. She had a minor graze on her head, and a sprained ankle. The SWAT team member will be out of ICU tomorrow, and should be discharged in a few more days."

Katie felt relieved that she hadn't let down the people she was responsible for, and that the injured man was recovering well. But she knew that wasn't why Andrews had called her in.

She waited to hear what it was.

Finally, he looked at her, intense.

"Katie, I need you to join an urgent meeting now. The FBI will be getting involved in an international investigation, and it's a strange one," Andrews said.

"What case is that?"

"A Canadian woman's body was found yesterday on the shores of Lake Ontario, near Four Mile Creek State Park. She was murdered. The circumstances are very concerning, as it appears to be a serial. We're about to have a briefing on it in the boardroom. Come this way."

A serial? Katie felt her heart quicken as she followed him into the boardroom.

Two men were sitting at the large, polished table, and they stood as she entered.

Andrews said, "Meet Special Agent Katie Winter. She's one of our top agents, who handled this morning's operation. Agent Winter, meet Detective Clark, and Detective Scott, who flew here earlier today from Toronto."

After handshakes all around, everyone sat down except Detective Clark, who stood at the head of the table.

"I'll start with some background," Clark said. "The man who found the body yesterday was ice fishing on Lake Ontario. He was looking across the ice when he saw a hair tie, covered in blood. Looking further, he saw a woman's body trapped in the ice. He called local police, who informed us yesterday evening. She's a Canadian citizen and resident, so her body must have been dumped on the Canadian side, and washed up on the US side."

Looking around the table, Katie saw everyone was looking serious as they took in this information.

Fascinating as the details were so far, it was the location which was sending chills down her spine. This body had been found in the Upper Peninsula. Where she had grown up. The one place in the world she had resolved never to go back to.

She was already dreading what was coming next.

"This is the second victim that has been found in the lake, in as many weeks. Both are women, and both were killed in a similar way," Clark explained. "That's why this is now an urgent matter."

"How did she die?" Katie asked.

"A combination of exposure and blood loss. Both were stabbed multiple times in the neck and chest with a sharp, bladed weapon. What makes the case significant is that both were found with a wooden chess piece in their mouth. This one was a knight. The pathologist found a wooden pawn lodged in the first victim's throat."

"What do you make of that?" Scott asked Katie.

"It's a signature," she said. "It's very typical of a serial killer crime and there are complex reasons for it. Sometimes, leaving a signature gives them a feeling of power. Sometimes, it is a display of pride in their kill."

Scott nodded.

"The chess pieces themselves? Any significance there?"

She nodded. "There will be, to the killer. It might be obvious, such as he's a chess player. Or it might be personal, something only he knows about."

Scott looked intrigued by what she'd said as he continued. "We can't find any other link between them. They lived in different cities and had completely different lives. Therefore, although we suspect a serial, we have no evidence or leads so far pointing to his or her identity."

Katie nodded. She knew that this was the most challenging and dangerous type of crime to solve, precisely because the criminals themselves were violent, unpredictable, and usually highly intelligent. Especially the 'organized' serial killers, who planned their crimes. Disorganized serial killers were more likely to kill at random. With the signatures left behind, and also the lack of any evidence so far, this had all the hallmarks of a case involving an organized serial killer.

"What about the first victim? Is she Canadian?" Katie asked.

"Both the victims are Canadian. The first victim lived in Toronto. She was found on the Canada side of the lake, to the east of Toronto. The most recent victim lived in Hamilton and was found in US territory."

"Are there any other similarities at all between the cases?"

"So far we haven't found any," Scott said.

"There must be common ground somewhere, surely?" Katie considered the possible thought processes of a serial killer. Feeling her way through their twisted mind was both fascinating and repelling. "Are they similar in age? Similar in appearance? Have you found any family or friends in common? What about work?"

"They are both blonde and blue eyed. Both young. Beyond that, they seem to have nothing in common."

"So that might be his chosen type," Katie thought aloud. "Of course, their looks could be just coincidental, and they might both be victims of opportunity. Being from such different areas, he may be picking a location, and then using that as a hunting ground."

"That's a possibility," Clark agreed. "We don't know nearly enough about the circumstances or the killer. But we need to get up to speed, and urgently. We are going to need cross-border cooperation, and an international task team, to solve this crime."

"We would like you to be part of the task team, Winter," Andrews said to her.

She stared at him in surprise.

"Why me?"

"We need an agent who is very familiar with the area, who knows its geography, and who understands the weather and can cope out in the wilderness. There's a massive cold front there now. And we also need someone with the experience and qualifications to work on a serial killer case. There aren't many agents with your level of expertise, or as respected as you. Your track record is stellar. We approached Andrews based on your experience, and when he said you had grown up in the Upper Peninsula area, we moved you to the top of our shortlist," Clark explained.

"We have three other agents on the list, but the agent who grew up in Rochester lacks serial killer experience, and the others haven't lived in that area. One was deployed in Buffalo for a year, but that's not enough time to gain the depth of local knowledge we need," Scott added.

"I grew up close to Wilson," Katie acknowledged. She vividly remembered the log house bordering Lake Ontario that had been her childhood home. Her father had run a small business hiring out fishing and sailing boats. He frequently had to go out and help lost or stranded customers, and as a result he was very familiar with the lake. Katie had accompanied him on many of those trips. The geography and details of the lake were etched in her memory.

So was the biting cold. She vividly remembered the months of ice. The restlessness she'd felt as winter refused to relinquish its grip. She'd yearned to live somewhere warmer even before the catastrophe had happened.

"Where will the team be based?" she asked.

"For now, it's based in Toronto, because these victims are Canadian, and we already have local police heavily involved on our side," Clark replied. "If you join us, you will be working alongside a unit of seasoned detectives. I will head up the team, and coordinate with the authorities across the border. We're still waiting for one more person, probably from the RCMP, to confirm. We'll endorse your passport so that you'll be free to cross the border as you need to."

In every way, Katie thought this seemed like an opportunity that she would jump at, but there were two big stumbling blocks.

The first was that she was already involved in a complex, dangerous case and she had a responsibility to her team. The second was that this serial killer case would take her back to her old home ground.

Katie hesitated. "You know my current case load, Andrews. Can I have time to think about this?"

Clark blinked in surprise, as if he'd expected her to say yes immediately. Scott frowned as if he, too, disapproved of her reply. Katie didn't care. She needed to do what she felt was right, and to be fully committed before she made her decision.

"The first task team meeting is tomorrow morning," Andrews said. "It's already five p.m. So we need your decision in an hour."

Katie nodded. "Thanks for all the background. I'll let you know in an hour. Now, if you'll excuse me, gents, I need to sign off on the paperwork for this morning's arrest."

She stood up, but to her surprise, Andrews walked with her to the boardroom door. Outside, he said to her in a quiet voice, "I know this may sound strange, but I sense joining this team will be good for you."

"In what way?" Katie asked, surprised that her boss was speaking to her on such a personal level.

"I know about the family tragedy you suffered when you were younger. I have a feeling you have some demons to face, and that this case will give you the chance to get closure," her boss said meaningfully.

His words shocked her. Katie would never have expected such an accurate insight from her usually unemotional and evidence-driven boss.

He was entirely right.

But the problem was, she didn't feel ready to face those demons.

CHAPTER FOUR

It was almost six p.m., fully dark, and chilly by the time Katie arrived home.

The apartment in downtown Chesapeake where she had lived for three years still looked much as it had the day she viewed it, give or take a few functional items of furniture. She hadn't added any personal touches. Hadn't taken many steps to make it feel like home.

She had moved into the apartment because it was in an ideal location for her purposes, affordable and convenient. She knew that she might have to relocate at any time. As an FBI agent she had learned not to get attached to any one place, as agents were moved around frequently.

She had few possessions apart from her work belongings and her clothes, but even those were limited. She didn't need much.

A minimalist, in all things, Katie knew this was a coping mechanism she had developed after the tragedy that had changed her life forever. She couldn't afford to be sentimental or emotional, but chose to keep herself apart from the world.

The large, openkitchen had granite worktops and stainless-steel appliances. The master bedroom was furnished simply. There was a door that led to the second bedroom, which she seldom opened. Her master bedroom had a balcony with a view of the bay – if she stood on tiptoes and peered around the neighboring high-rise.

The furniture in the apartment was modern and functional. Nothing else was needed. It was simply a place to sleep and sometimes to eat. Work took priority in her life. In fact, Katie thought, her job was her only passion.

She hung her coat on the hook inside the front door, and took off her shoes, placing them on the rack below and slipping her feet into a pair of old, comfortable sneakers. Returning to the kitchen, she opened the fridge and poured herself a glass of wine.

With a sigh, perching on the stool at the counter, she sipped. It was time to confront the decision that was hanging over her because the hour she'd been given was now over.

Should she take the offer and join the task force hunting the killer in the Upper Peninsula?

It would mean leaving her current team, and the case she was busy with. And it would mean revisiting the shores of the lake where she'd grown up. The place she never again wanted to think of as home after the tragedy of her twin sister, Josie.

Her twin's disappearance had left an ugly scar on her soul, and Katie knew she would be forever haunted by the questions.

She'd worked so hard to erase the pain and guilt and anger, but had found herself unable to return to the hometown where she might find answers.

Eventually, Katie had decided that her best coping mechanism was simply to bury herself in work and not to think about the past at all.

She hadn't talked about her sister with anyone apart from having a couple of unrewarding sessions with a psychologist, a few years ago. Although Katie had hoped that they might help to erase the pain she felt, they hadn't done much. Perhaps that was because she hadn't told the shrink the whole truth. She feared, deeply, that Josie hadn't died in the white-water rafting accident, but that something worse had happened to her.

Her twin had disappeared. Her body had never been found. Katie had never stopped feeling deeply guilty about the pain and heartache she'd caused.

She was responsible for Josie's fate. She was the one who'd recklessly suggested they go out when the water was too rough. Katie had talked Josie into it. Practically forced her, in fact.

Her twin's life jacket had been discovered the next day, hooked on a tree branch, but her body had never been found.

She knew that returning to the lake would bring back the memories and that she would not be able to stop herself from exploring her worst fears.

Even now, she didn't know if she was ready.

Trying to convince herself to make the right decision, Katie reminded herself that two women had recently died. Was she going to let other families experience pain and grief without any closure?

At that moment, her phone rang.

It was Andrews on the line. It was crunch time now, and Katie knew she couldn't delay any longer. She picked up the call, thinking once again about what she'd be getting into.

Andrews sounded stressed and tired, as if he'd had a long day.

"Agent Winter," he said. "Have you made your decision yet?"

Katie took a deep breath. In the moment, she decided she was going to stay with her current team.

"I don't want to leave the case I'm busy with. The answer is no," she said regretfully.

There was a short silence. She heard Andrews's heavy sigh. Then he cleared his throat in a purposeful way. Her boss, determined and dedicated and sometimes stubborn to a fault, was not taking her immediate refusal for an answer.

"Not even if I told you to check your personal feelings at the door?" Andrews asked. "After all, you're a professional."

Those words stung, but Katie did her best to reply calmly.

"It wouldn't be fair to my team if I drop them," Katie said. "And also, I don't want my personal feelings and background to compromise the task force. Not after my twin's disappearance, and the circumstances surrounding it."

"I know what you must have gone through." Now Andrews sounded surprisingly sympathetic. Katie didn't know what to say in reply, so there was a short silence before Andrews continued.

"It takes a special kind of person to do this job. Not many people have experienced what you have, or fought the way you have done. I know what happened was traumatizing. But it's shaped you into a person who can add real value to this team."

"Thank you," she said. "I appreciate your words. But that doesn't mean I want to go back to my hometown. I've moved on; I've found peace."

Andrews argued back. "This could be solved fast. You might be away only a week or two. Maybe even less time than that."

Katie sighed. "If it was anywhere else on the planet, I'd reconsider. You know that, Andrews."

"If it was any other assignment on the planet, I'd send someone else," her boss shot back. "This murder happened yesterday. Once the media picks up on it, it's going to explode. We're going to be under huge pressure to solve it. If this fails, then people are going to start asking why you didn't go, and we'll both get the backlash for it."

Katie tapped her fingers on the counter as she considered his words. She had to admit, this argument hit home. Ever since she had been transferred to Virginia, Andrews had impressed her with his tough, fair-minded approach. He'd been in her corner when she'd needed his backup. She liked him and respected him deeply. Now he was directly asking for her help.

"And don't be worried about your current caseload. We'll fly another agent in, if needed. We'll make sure that if you join the task force, your team has all the support they need," Andrews appealed.

Setting out the positives so clearly reminded Katie that this would be a true test of her ability, as well as her dedication to the job, and her loyalty to Agent Andrews.

It was also worth considering the negatives, Katie thought, even though she didn't like to dwell on them. She knew that as a female field agent in the FBI, she would always need to try harder to prove herself and think about her career future. Refusing to join the task force hunting down a dangerous serial killer would not be well received.

"Two women have been murdered, Winter," Andrews said softly, providing her with the final words in his argument. "You could stop it from happening again."

That, more than anything, was the deciding factor that changed her mind.

If she had a chance of stopping this killing spree, she had to try. Otherwise more families would be broken and traumatized, just as hers had been.

She closed her eyes and sighed. Sooner or later, the time would come to face her demons.

One is never ready, she had once heard someone say, in a support meeting. *And the time is always too soon. Wait for the perfect time, and you'll be waiting all your life.*

She wasn't ready. And the time wasn't right.

But the time, she realized, would never be right.

She took one last deep breath.

"All right," she said decisively. "I'm in."

CHAPTER FIVE

Katie stared out of the window as the plane touched down, the wheels spinning on the icy runway. Toronto Pearson airport was blanketed in snow and watching it, she shivered.

She hadn't brought much luggage with her, just her purse and a small carry-on with basic toiletries and a couple of changes of clothes. But despite the meagerness of her possessions, Katie felt resolute as the plane taxied to the airport. Now that she had taken the first step, and was on Canadian soil, she knew it had been the right decision to come here.

She stood up, watching the other passengers as they shuffled into line. Some were definitely commuting for work on this cold Wednesday morning, dressed in somber suits and dark coats, carrying laptop bags and briefcases.

Others were families. With a surprising sense of longing, she stared at the mother with two daughters in the seats in front of her. Dark haired and pretty, the girls looked about twelve years old and were also twins. Again, her thoughts veered painfully to Josie.

The moment she stepped off the plane, Katie's face was stung by the arctic cold. It almost took her breath away, and she was glad she had a scarf wrapped around her neck.

She hadn't experienced this level of cold in more than ten years, and it brought back memories of her childhood in the ice and snow. Building snowmen. Sledding with Josie. Rushing through the frigid wind to get from the house to the car.

Shivering, Katie tried her best to ignore these thoughts and focus on the task at hand.

She wasn't going to let the cold get to her, and nor was she going to let the memories get to her.

She was going to be the best she could be, and solve this case for Josie, and for the other families that had been forever scarred by the tragedy of these murders.

The sky outside was a clear, piercing blue although Katie knew the strong wind could blow in changeable weather at any time. The snow on the ground had been packed down by the passing of many sets of wheels and footprints. She had to shield her eyes from the low, dazzling glare in order to see where she was going.

She hurried into the airport building, which was a warm, buzzing hive of activity. After passing through immigration, with no checked in baggage to claim, Katie walked straight out to Arrivals, looking out for whoever would be there to meet her.

Scanning the waiting faces, she saw a tall, slim man, with a shock of gray hair, waving at her. She recognized Detective Scott from the meeting the previous day, and she felt glad to see him again. She wondered if she would be partnered with him on this investigation.

“Good to see you, Agent Winter," Scott said, as he shook her hand. “Where's your bag?"

"I don't have one. I travel light," she admitted.

Scott nodded, looking surprised but approving, and led the way out of the airport.

"We're going to go straight to the Toronto police headquarters," he explained. "We have a meeting in half an hour to discuss the case. You'll be able to meet all the others involved and I'll introduce you to your case partner. He was wrapping up a murder case yesterday, so couldn’t join us."

"That sounds great," Katie said, feeling eager to learn more details, and meet the team.

*

The Toronto Police Headquarters were located downtown, in a large, nondescript building that looked like any other government building in any other city in the world. The parking lot was protected by a large, heavy gate. A guard opened the gate and directed them to a parking spot.

They took the elevator to the fourth floor and Scott led the way to a meeting room with a big wooden table and eight black leather chairs.

Four men were seated. Katie immediately recognized Clark, the Canadian detective who she had met the previous day. He stood as soon as she walked in, and hurried over to shake her hand.

"This is FBI Special Agent Katie Winter," he introduced her. "Meet the rest of the team."

The other men stood up. They were all older than her, in their forties or fifties and early sixties, except for one dark haired man who she guessed to be in his mid-thirties. She moved around the table, shaking hands with each of them.

"This is police psychologist Chris Johnson," the Canadian detective introduced him. "He has worked with us on several cases in the past. This is Detective Damien Anderson from the Toronto Police Department. And this is your case partner," Scott introduced the dark-haired man in his mid-thirties. "Detective Antoine Leblanc has a strong background in investigation and forensics. You two will be working together on all aspects of the case."

Antoine Leblanc didn't look as pleased to see her as she expected. In fact, Katie thought her new case partner's greeting was as frosty as the wintry weather they had just driven through. Not even the trace of a smile warmed his strong, olive-skinned features. She was worried that it would prove difficult to work with him. Having a cooperative case partner would be vital for solving this challenging serial crime.

Katie shook the man's hand firmly after slipping her carry-on from her shoulder to rest it on the floor. "It's good to meet you, Detective Leblanc."

"Likewise, Agent Winter," he said, but he didn't return her smile.

"All right, let's start by going over the details of the case and establishing some parameters," Clark said, opening a laptop and projecting images onto the screen as the team hurriedly took their seats.

Katie couldn't wait to get to work, and she began to mentally sort out the information she had been given.

"Two women, both blondes, murdered two weeks apart. Both crimes followed the same modus operandi which I believe you know?" He raised his eyebrows at Katie, who nodded, remembering the stabbings that had been described to her with the bodies dumped into the lake.

"The victims themselves are quite different," Clark then said. "The first victim was a woman called Elizabeth Martin, twenty-three years old, who was employed at a fashion boutique in Toronto. She lived on her own and used to enjoy hiking in the wilderness. She was reported missing after she didn't arrive at work on Monday. Her body was found a couple of days later," he explained.

Katie stared at the image of the smiling blonde, feeling a sense of deep sadness. Photos always got to her. At that moment in time, this happy girl had no idea what horror awaited her. This was why Katie felt so passionate about her job. She couldn't erase what had already been done, but she could prevent others suffering the same fate.

"This is the second victim, Christine Harrison," Scott continued, sending the image of a pretty, long-haired girl onto the screen. "She was a junior at McMaster University in Hamilton, Ontario, but she was struggling academically and had a drugs problem that she was seeking help for. She had an on-off relationship with a boyfriend who she stayed with, but he was in Ottawa the whole week for a sales conference, so has a confirmed alibi. It also means they don't know exactly when she disappeared, as he was away, and she skipped class frequently. She wasn't a lover of outdoor activities, and her boyfriend and friends have said they have no idea how she would have ended up in the lake area."

More photos followed in quick succession. Photos of the bodies. The stillness of death, and the paleness of their skin. Both of the women's bodies had been frozen into the ice. Both had their clothing stripped away. The nude female flesh on display was not a sight for the faint of heart, although it wasn't suggestive in any way.

Scott kept the photos coming. Two women. Frozen in ice. Helpless in death. He'd included close-ups of the chess pieces as they were found in the victims' mouths, and also once they were removed.

Katie narrowed her eyes. This sight was more difficult to accept than she'd thought it would be. Why had he done such a thing, she wondered, seeking refuge in logical thought as she strove to understand this killer's twisted mind.

Scott's voice was flat as he added, "There were no signs of a struggle, no defensive marks. The bodies were very well preserved. There is no doubt that this is a serial killer. We'll have a better idea of the MO once we run the DNA results."

"The chess pieces, we believe are signatures," Johnson said and Katie nodded, glad to have the psychologist on the team confirm her theory.

However, the detectives were frowning. There was a scarcity of evidence on this case. What had happened? How had the killer made contact? These were questions that couldn't yet be answered.

"The most important question, for me, is when the killer will strike again," she said, and the others nodded in grim agreement.

"If the killer is operating according to a time interval, and Christine Harrison was killed recently, then we might have time, although some serial killers do speed up their intervals," she explained. "But if Christine Harrison was killed earlier in the week, then the killer might be preparing to strike again at any moment."

How could she try to predict what was triggering his kills? Perhaps looking at the site might give her a clue.

"Can I go and view the scene where the first body was found?" she asked.

Scott nodded. "Sure. Take a drive out there with Detective Leblanc. He also mentioned he'd like to have a look as soon as possible."

Katie didn't miss Leblanc's frown. Her new partner seemed angry about having her on this case. She thought he resented her, but had no idea why.

She hoped she might find out, on the drive to the icy wilderness.

CHAPTER SIX

Katie hurried out of the police headquarters, a few steps behind the unsmiling Leblanc, who was walking as fast as his long legs would allow, and at a speed that made any conversation impossible.

Heading out into the bitter cold, Leblanc walked to a dark SUV parked across the street. Although the police headquarters was a modern, functional building, Katie noticed other, historic buildings nearby that caught her eye with their decorative and eclectic style. Intrigued, she stopped for a better look despite the knife-like wind.

Seeing Leblanc staring at her irritably, she quickly climbed into the car. There, Katie decided she had to try and break the ice between herself and her new partner.

"How long have you been in the Toronto headquarters?" she asked Leblanc.

He was silent for a moment, then said, "A year."

His voice was deep. She picked up a tinge of a French accent in it. The answer was short and to the point, and confirmed to Katie that the man wasn't exactly the most talkative of individuals. Not to her, at any rate.

Had he been with the Toronto police force all along? Maybe he'd been in the army. He had that no-nonsense soldier look about him. Except that she didn't think that his manner was that of a soldier. The army would have taught him to be more polite, more respectful of his superiors, so to speak.

"I didn't realize you were so new to the city," she said. "Where were you before that?"

"Quebec."

“Were you born there?”

“Yes. But I spent most of my life in Paris, France. I returned for family reasons,” he said.

“Paris!” That was a city Katie had always wanted to visit. She would have loved to ask what it was like working as a detective in this historic, romantic European destination but decided now wasn’t the time.

"So you came back, and then transferred from Quebec to Toronto," she said.

"Yes." He sounded even grumpier now.

"You don't sound too happy about it."

"It's nothing to do with being transferred," he shrugged.

"Do you have experience in serial killer cases?" Katie asked.

She'd honestly meant the question to be conversational, but Leblanc didn't take it well. His frown deepened.

"I have experience in violent crimes and forensics," he shot back. "Our team is highly qualified."

She wasn't sure what to make of Leblanc's terse replies. Did he always speak so little, or was he just angry that the FBI was involved?

At any rate, she was tired of the one-word answers and decided to give up trying to make conversation. If Leblanc didn't want to make small talk with her, she was damned if she was going to force him.

To her surprise, Katie found that his unhelpful attitude was making her feel even more determined to crack this case in the shortest time. Perhaps she was as contrary as he was in her own way, she thought, surprising herself with a touch of humor.

Instead of pushing ahead with small talk, she looked out of the window, mesmerized by the scenery that was unfolding as they drove out of the city and into the wilderness.

Leaving the city behind, they drove through vast, snow-covered fields, with the odd stand of trees in the distance, standing out dark and skeletal against the white landscape.

Katie felt at once comforted and threatened by the vast expanse of frozen wasteland. It was hard to believe that, in spring, it would be full of color. Right now it was beautiful, Katie decided, in a stark, wild and very cold way.

Leblanc turned off the main road, and they were soon driving along a narrow path that wound between large mounds of snow.

Glancing at the sky, Katie was dismayed to see that the weather was changing. Clouds were looming from the north. They looked dark and heavy with snow, and she knew that it was only a matter of time before the weather would close in.

Her mind veered once again to the case. It was a closed book: a mystery. How had the crimes played out? How had this killer chosen his victims? The possibilities chilled her. With no common threads, it would be impossible to predict who he might target next, or how soon he would strike.

"Here we are," said Leblanc gruffly, interrupting her musings. He stopped the SUV at the end of the track.

Ahead of her, she saw a couple of small wooden huts and shelters, and beyond was the vast expanse of Lake Ontario. Climbing out of the car, Katie took in the look and feel of this deserted scene.

She was struck by how bleak it was. In this arctic landscape of snow and barren trees, the frozen lake gleamed an icy, foreboding white.

She thought back on the details of the reports from the two murder sites.

"You think she was killed here?" Katie said to Leblanc. "Or killed elsewhere and transported here? Was there any sign of a struggle by the lake?"

He shrugged, pulling his woolen hat further down over his dark hair.

"There had been a recent snowfall," he said. "Not even vehicle tracks were visible."

"And at the other site?"

"It was the same. No evidence. Snow hiding everything."

He still sounded grumpy. Katie suspected it was more because of her presence here with him than because of the lack of evidence.

With her muscles aching from the cold, she carefully made her way down the embankment, wondering how easy it would have been to carry a body down this slippery, icy path. Of course, it might have been no easier to drag a struggling victim along. How had this played out? There was so much they needed to know.

"The body was found there." Leblanc pointed.

"Frozen into the ice?" Katie asked.

Leblanc nodded.

Katie stood at the edge of the lake, watching snowflakes dance and swirl around her.

"This is such a stark, desolate place. Does that reflect his mindset? Did he want to create a scenario where he was alone with her?" she said aloud. Instinctively, she felt that was important. Perhaps this killer was socially awkward, craving an intimate relationship but unable to achieve it.

Leblanc wrapped his arms around himself, looking as if he'd had enough of standing in the wind and listening to Katie theorize.

But at that moment, another thought occurred to Katie. Perhaps it wasn't only the deserted location that was important. The snow covering all tracks was also a noticeable feature of the site. What if this was his modus operandi?

“The snow was very convenient for him. This killer seems to be a careful planner. He might be waiting for the next snowfall to kill again,” she said. “That might be what he’s using as his interval. If so, it means we don’t have much time.” She stared up at the gathering clouds.

Leblanc drew in a sharp breath. Now he, too, looked worried.

"Forensics might know more about the time of death by now. Let's go to the pathologist’s office, and view the bodies,” he said.

*

The icy wind scoured Katie’s numb cheeks as she and Leblanc trudged up the paved path toward the large building that housed the forensic pathology headquarters.

Inside, the pathologist and his assistant were waiting in the lobby, along with a couple of other members of the team.

"This is Dr. Richard Selleck," Leblanc introduced them. "This is FBI agent Katie Winter."

"Please, mask and gown up here and we can go through to the autopsy rooms. You can view the bodies there, and I will talk you through what I found," Dr. Selleck said.

Katie put on her mask and gown, pulling the tie rope and straightening out the long sleeves.

She then followed Selleck into a white tiled room with a large metal table at the center. The fluorescent lights gave the room an eerie glow.

The bodies were laid out on the table, covered with white sheets.

Dr. Selleck pulled back the sheets to reveal the face of the first victim.

Katie's breath caught in her throat as she saw the deep stab wounds in the young woman's neck, and the wooden chess piece, which had been placed next to her corpse. She stared at the table for a long moment.

How she wished that she could see what this dead woman had seen; that she could look out from her eyes and recognize her killer's face. Had he felt pleasure as he cut and stabbed her? Why had he left that chess piece as his signature?

"This is the second victim." Selleck moved to the next table.

As the sheets were pulled back, Katie was surprised by the similarity between the two victims.

Both women had been attractive. They had the same delicate features, the same blue eyes and long, bright blond hair. Was he choosing the victims based on their hair? Now that she could see the two side by side, this made more sense. Perhaps that was what was attracting him, like a moth to a flame.

“We cannot determine whether the cause of death in both cases was loss of blood, exposure, or a combination of the two," Selleck said. "There was no evidence of rape, and no wounds below the heart area."

"What about the time of death? Could the bodies have been dumped at an earlier time, before the lake froze?" Katie asked.

Selleck shook his head. "No. Forensically, it's more likely they were dumped recently, just as the snow was falling and the lake was freezing up."

Katie shivered. This backed up her theory that the killer was using the cold snaps and the snowfalls to time his murders, knowing his tracks would be covered.

She stared uneasily through the double-glazed window of the lab. Outside, from the darkening sky, the first flakes were beginning to flutter down. That meant, if her theory was right, it would soon be time for him to strike again.

“We’re running out of time,” Leblanc said, echoing her thoughts, even though she thought he was more focused on the practicalities of the weather than the killer’s cycle. “Christine Harrison’s parents live near here. If we’re going to interview them today, we’d better hurry.”

“Let’s go,” Katie agreed.

CHAPTER SEVEN

The watcher stood on the main street in Watertown, New York. His fists were bunched tightly inside his woolen gloves, but he was too absorbed to be aware of the cold.

Inside the well-lit window, the busy doctors' rooms looked like a different world from the stark, cold sidewalk outside. The blonde receptionist behind the desk smiled, greeting a patient, pushing her hair back as she turned to the computer. She looked closely at the screen, her fingers tapping over the keyboard fast and expertly. She turned to the printer, took a page from it, passed it to the patient with another friendly smile.

It was her hair that had first caught his eye yesterday when he had passed by. The flash of gold had attracted him and drawn him to her.

Now, he felt a sense of inevitability as he observed her, as if he was watching a scene play out. A scene in a movie, but one he would only be allowed to view, and couldn't be part of at all, even if he tried.

"You're beautiful," he whispered.

Then he tried again, louder, surprised by the strength in his own voice.

"Hey! You're beautiful!"

She didn't see him even though he felt as if his stare was burning through her. She was like a movie star. The heroine in her own life, and what a beautiful life it was. Look how that elderly man was smiling at her! And there was the doctor, rushing out of his rooms.

She glanced toward the doctor and smiled. The doctor grinned back, his lips mouthing words that the watcher couldn't understand because the glass was thick and insulated and he could not lip read. But both she and the patient laughed.

It was a joke that he was not part of. Excluded from. They didn't know he was watching, and even if they knew, they would not see him. He was gray and invisible. A nobody in their life.

She glanced out of the window but her eyes passed over him as if he wasn't even there at all.

It was his own fault, he thought, that he was living his life so cut off from the world.

He was clever, with a piercing intelligence that allowed him to do things others couldn't. But he couldn't fit in with others. He couldn't understand them. Not in the way he needed to. Their normality confused him but when he tried to share what was in his mind, others became frightened and repelled by him. He had tried, so many times, but each time he found himself confined to the same role.

All he could do was look and watch.

He felt a sudden, intense rush of hatred toward this blonde princess, so confident and beautiful. How dare she ignore him! She was like all the others, and she would deserve everything that came her way.

Perhaps she was laughing at his expense, and the doctor was joining in. Laughing at him too. He felt furious with them both. They were playing games with him. The doctor said something else, and she laughed, louder now, pushing back that glorious hair. She looked so beautiful as she laughed.

He could see her teeth, her bright white teeth.

He had thought she would be caring, this pretty woman, working for a doctor. Why wasn't she showing him the sympathy and attention he'd expected?

He hadn't gotten it from the woman in the fashion boutique, even though he'd gone in and pretended to be a potential customer. She'd looked at him strangely as he'd fumbled through the brightly colored scarves while clumsily trying to start up a conversation. She'd stepped back as if she didn't want him there.

And then he'd seen the student. Troubled and needy. She should have seen him, too. She should have been drawn to him as one of her own kind. But she had looked at him fearfully, as if she could see his darkest secrets.

And now, this woman, too, was ignoring him.

His mind flashed back to what had happened when he was younger. How it had felt to be locked away and abandoned. The distant memories were deeply suppressed so that even he could only get glimpses.

Panic rose up in him again. He felt his breath coming out in quick, sharp bursts. He looked around him. So many people, hurrying past him, their eyes looking straight ahead. He thought of the woman in the café who hadn't even noticed him. The one who'd climbed into her car as he was climbing out, without a glance at him.

"Hey," he called out. "Hey, look at me. Look at me! Look at me!"

But nobody did. Not the passers-by, swathed in their heavy coats, now giving him a wide berth. And not the blonde inside, who must have seen him by now, but perhaps she had not.

At that moment, the watcher made up his mind to kill her. His lips pressed together in resolve. It was time. It had to be done.

His breath misted in the cold air as his mind churned with images and thoughts of the hours ahead – of how he would do it and when. He needed to make it so perfect, so that nobody would ever know that he had touched her life, and then taken it.

The woman looked up at the clock. He could see that she was still working, albeit more slowly now. Winding down to the end of her working day, he guessed she was waiting for six p.m. to leave. At six, it would be completely dark.

A snowflake fluttered down, surprising him with its cold kiss on his face. He brushed it away and looked up into the leaden sky. A storm was coming. He had felt it in the air earlier, but now the first flakes were beginning to fall.

He shivered, moving closer to the window. It was beginning to snow harder. He could hear it swirling in the air, the faint swish and rattle like distant fairy wings.

The killer moved closer, inhaling the fumes from the exhaust pipe of a departing car. She was packing up now. She would leave the medical rooms and take the elevator down to the basement parking. He knew she would be hurrying, wanting to get home before the snowfall started in earnest.

He knew she lived alone.

Above the torment in his soul, he felt a strange elation that this beautiful, confident woman would soon pay for her arrogance, her superiority, and for the sins of all the other women who had so often ignored him.

The young woman quickly gathered her belongings and walked towards the back door of the clinic. He felt the adrenaline rush, a familiar feeling from what he thought of as his previous life, when he'd done different things, before he'd capitulated and let his true nature take over.

He pulled the heavy woolen muffler up over his nose, his eyes still fixed on the woman. He was excited, because this was his chance to make things right for himself, to get revenge at last. He was already imagining her terror, her pleading. Begging for her life.

Reaching into his pocket, he felt the chess piece he'd put there earlier. The small, wooden object made his mind shift in strange ways as he touched it, turning it over and over.

Turning purposefully away from the window and heading to the basement's exit, he resolved that she would suffer in turn, just as he had done while watching her.

Only then would she understand his pain.

CHAPTER EIGHT

Christine Harrison's mother lived in Hamilton, on the opposite side of the city from McMaster University. When Katie and Leblanc pulled up outside the estate, her first thought was that it was depressing.

A large, sprawling, featureless estate of double-story housing, it was surrounded mostly by flat, snow-covered grounds. Gazing around, Katie picked up a children's play area set on a concrete square in the far distance. The bright yellow of the slide was the only splash of color in this gray estate, set against a dark and looming sky.

She tried to visualize how growing up in this setting had affected the young, pretty and troubled Christine. As a teen in these grim and colorless surrounds, Christine must have longed for adventure. But her search for color and excitement, rebelling against the uniform grayness, had taken her in the wrong direction. It had set her on a road that had led to drug abuse and personal problems.

"I'm sure you can buy drugs here without even leaving the estate," Katie said sadly to Leblanc as they pulled into the parking.

Leblanc gave a terse nod. Katie had no idea if it was in agreement or disapproval. Yet again, she thought to herself that her investigation partner sure hadn't been chosen for his conversational abilities.

Leblanc parked the car, and they got out. She could feel the bite of the winter air in her lungs as they walked up to Building 12. It felt surprisingly quiet. The softly falling flakes created an expectant hush.

"Liz Harrison lives on the second floor. Apartment 225," Katie said.

This interview would be hard. Liz Harrison had lost her only daughter and would still be devastated and in shock. Katie knew what it was like to lose a close family member, to have them disappear from your life forever. The pain never went away but at this early point it would be unbearable. Agony would be consuming Liz. Katie would need to be sensitive and sympathetic, while striving to get as much information as she could from the grieving mother.

They made their way up the remaining flight of stairs and approached apartment 225. Katie pushed the doorbell and a shrill, piercing sound echoed in her ears.

A woman who looked to be in her early fifties came to the door. Her brown hair was thin and stick-straight and she wore a gray coat over a gray skirt. Her face was anxious and drawn, and her eyes were swollen and red. Staring at the agents, wringing her hands together, Katie thought she looked exhausted, as if their presence was too much for her, at such a time.

She felt deep regret and sympathy for her. At the same time, she was uneasily aware that if the killer continued with his spree, then more parents would be in the same heartbreaking predicament. She had no choice but to push forward and find out what the mother knew.

"Mrs. Harrison?" Katie asked gently.

The woman nodded, but didn't answer.

"I'm FBI Special Agent Katie Winter, and this is Detective Leblanc. I'm sorry to have to ask questions at such a difficult time."

"Come in," Liz said, her voice hoarse and ragged.

The small apartment was a mess. Clothes were strewn over the sagging sofas. Beyond, Katie saw the small kitchen was cluttered with dirty dishes. The air smelled stale, and harsh with cigarette smoke. Katie guessed this had been a chaotic and depressing place even before her daughter's death. Now it was worse.

On the mantelpiece, there were a few pictures of Christine. Some were school photos of a smiling, blond child in front of the school's banner. There were a couple of shots of her in a garden, against a summer sky. Katie noticed that none of the pictures were recent.

"I'm so sorry about Christine," Katie said sympathetically. Beside her, Leblanc nodded solemnly.

"It's devastating! My daughter, gone." Liz wiped her eyes with shaking hands. "I know she had her problems. I worried, time to time, that something might happen. But I never dreamed it would be this."

"When was the last time you saw her?" Katie asked.

"Two days ago."

"Did she come here?"

Liz looked down. "With her boyfriend away, she came over. She borrowed some cash. She was short of money for food. She didn't stay long."

With a pang, Katie knew that Liz knew the requested money had not been intended for food. Had a drug deal gone wrong, she wondered. Was this killer somehow connected to this shady underworld?

"I'm sure she did keep a lot of her life from you, Mrs. Harrison. But we were wondering what you could tell us about her friends and her contacts."

"Christine didn't have many friends. Not that I knew of. She was more of a loner. She left home a year and a half ago, and I don't know many of the people she associated with since then."

"Did she keep in touch with school friends? And college friends, at the university? Did anyone ever come around here looking for her or asking about her?"

"Nobody came here. I don't know what to tell you. I don't understand." Liz burst into tears. "Why her? Why my Christine?"

Up until now they had all been standing in the small lounge. It had felt awkward, but they hadn't been invited to sit on any of the cluttered chairs. Now, Liz collapsed onto a threadbare armchair and buried her face in her hands.

Katie exchanged a glance with Leblanc. She didn't think the mother had any useful information. She had been estranged from her daughter. Her daughter had been involved in circles she hadn't been part of. She'd been dabbling in the drug underworld, but if that had led to her death, they would have to seek the information elsewhere.

Uneasily, she glanced out of the small window. The snow was starting to fall heavier now, and thoughts of the killer crowded into her mind again. It was getting dark outside.

"Did she have any enemies you know of? Anyone she was fighting with or having problems with? Do you have any idea who could have wanted to hurt her?" Katie asked once Liz had blown her nose.

Liz shook her head. "No. No one!"

"Did she mention any plans?"

Liz shook her head. "No."

"How did she seem when you spoke to her?"

"She sounded the way she has recently. Not happy. She was a troubled person." Liz sighed.

"Was she with anyone when she visited you?" Leblanc asked. Katie was surprised by the gentleness in his voice. She hadn't thought her case partner had much empathy. Perhaps she was wrong.

Liz shook her head. "No. She came here alone. She kept her life from me. I think she was afraid I would judge her." Liz's face was drained of color. She took a shuddering breath. "She kept messing up, with the drugs and the problems, and she started to think that I hated her. I told her that wasn't true, but she wouldn't believe me. She just got worse and worse and then she just packed up and left." Liz paused and stared into space for a moment.

"Did you know who she used drugs with, or where she bought from?" Katie said. "Did you know whether she was going to visit any of her connections, any dealers, after coming here?"

Liz shook her head. "When she came here the last time, she said she wasn't doing that anymore. She told me that she was finished with it."

"Did you believe her?"

Liz shrugged. "I don't know. Maybe."

Katie guessed that Liz had been hopeful.

"I never knew the truth anymore with her. She lied to me. She lied to me so often!" Liz continued.

"I'm sorry," Katie put a hand on Liz's shoulder. Her body was shaking.

Leblanc shifted from foot to foot, looking awkward and concerned.

" I think we should go," said Katie. "Please, take care. Can you call someone to be with you? You shouldn't have to be alone right now."

Liz nodded. "I – I will do that. Will try to."

As they left, before Leblanc closed the door quietly behind them, Katie heard the sound of sobs behind her again. She shivered. Liz was clearly a broken woman. But she didn't know anything about her daughter that could lead them further.

Katie knew that it was all too easy for someone you loved to fall through the cracks. It had been too late for Liz to have changed anything, but she guessed, sadly, that there had never been the chance. Christine had chosen her own road in life, and chosen badly. But Katie still wasn't sure if her choices had led to her death.

However, this gut-wrenching visit had given them more clarity on the murder's timeline. Just as she had this thought, Leblanc voiced it.

"Christine last contacted her mother two days ago. That confirms what the coroner said," he observed as they walked back to the car. Katie noticed that he was speaking in his normal sharp, clipped tone once again, the sympathy gone. "She was killed immediately and dumped. Not held captive."

Katie nodded. "It gives us a clearer idea of the modus operandi."

"Perhaps he lured his victims to the place where they were killed," Leblanc observed as he started up the car and Katie knew he was thinking again of how vulnerable Christine would have been. Open to any promise of something better.

Dark clouds were smothering the sky and the snow was coming in freezing gusts. They rushed to the car and got inside as quickly as they could.

"I don't think he could have lured them there," she said, knowing it would irritate Leblanc. Sure enough, he frowned immediately.

"Why?" he sounded ready for an argument.

"I think if he killed them quickly, he took them the same way. He just grabbed them and ran. Perhaps he got into their house, or waited for them to come home."

"There was no sign of a struggle in their homes, according to the police report," Leblanc countered, angry now.

"There wouldn't need to be," Katie explained patiently. "The point is that I don't think the killer wanted to know these victims at all. Based on this timeline, I get the feeling he's not killing them for who they are. He doesn't want to know them. Being similar looking, they might represent something to him."

"You think?" Leblanc sounded less argumentative now and as if he was finally understanding her logic.

"I wonder if, in his mind, he's killing someone else. Over and over again," Katie said.

"He started with Elizabeth Martin," Leblanc said. "Why her?"

Katie nodded. "Why was she the first? That could be important, as there might have been some kind of connection with the first victim. Let's go talk to her parents now."

CHAPTER NINE

Gaby Mackay hated being the last person to leave the clinic. Being alone gave her the creeps, but it was the receptionist's job to lock up.

It had been a long day in the clinic, she thought, closing the door. Some days, she felt tired of this job. On days like today, she felt motivated to quit and go into something different. Maybe get out of Watertown, with its small-town banality and endless winters, and make a fresh start elsewhere.

She felt conflicted, because she'd recently met Craig. He worked at the auto parts store and was a cool guy. He seemed to like her. But there was also the semi-flirtation she had with Doctor Nathan in the clinic. He was in his early thirties and divorced, but that wasn't so much of an age gap. She was twenty-three.

Flirty Doctor Nathan was moving to Florida soon, and he had hinted strongly that there would be an opportunity there for her. Problem was, she didn't know if he was serious – about her, or the Florida offer.

Tonight she was seeing Craig. This would be their second date and she'd get an idea, from here, about where things were going with him. She'd be able to make a decision then. Checking the time, Gaby saw she had only half an hour to get ready before meeting him in a bar downtown.

She walked downstairs and through the quiet basement that was freezing cold year-round but particularly arctic in winter.

As Gaby walked toward her car, she glanced behind her. Only a couple of cars remained in the basement. The only sounds were the swish of traffic outside, and a dripping noise from somewhere closer. It was dark and cold and for some reason she felt spooked.

She hadn't felt comfortable today. She'd felt as if someone had been watching her, although that could just have been because creepy Mr. Barnard was there for his monthly meds. Mr. Barnard was pushing seventy and he loved to lean across the reception desk and squeeze her arm. Katie thought it was an excuse to look down her blouse.

Mr. Barnard had reminded her of the other patient who had given her a hard time a month or two ago. That guy had made her feel seriously uneasy, with his attempts at flirting, and the narrow-eyed way he had looked at her, and the moment when he'd actually leaned over the counter and tried to stroke her hair.

That was probably what it was, she decided, climbing in and starting up. Mr. Barnard had reminded her of that uncomfortable harassment.

It was starting to snow hard. She might have to stay home tonight, Gaby thought as she drove out of the basement, worried by how the flakes were starting to pour down onto her windshield.

She hated driving in the snow. That was another reason to move to Florida, she decided, turning in the direction of home, which was a cottage on the edge of town. Narrowing her eyes against the falling flakes, she headed down the road, thankful it wasn't a long drive.

She passed the lights of the main house, where her landlord lived, and continued beyond. Easing the car along the snow-packed driveway that only she used, she parked in the cottage's small garage. She climbed out, and hurried around to the front door, shivering as she unlocked it, the flakes tickling her hair.

Her phone rang as she entered the cozy cottage. Pulling off her coat and unwinding her scarf, Gaby hesitated and let it ring, not really in the mood for a conversation. But it could be Craig changing their meet-up. She pulled the phone out of her purse, rolling her eyes as she saw it was her bossy older sister, Fiona.

Fiona was five years older than her. She was married and settled and seemingly disapproved of every breath Gaby took.

"Hey, Fi."

"Gaby. We have a family dinner tonight. Peter's dad is in town. Can you come?"

“Tonight?” Gaby heard the incredulity in her own voice. Peter was Fiona's husband. He wasn't her family. Fiona just needed her to make up the numbers so they could be a table of four.

“I'm busy. I have a date just now,” she said.

"Really? Who with?" Irritated, Gaby knew she'd used the wrong excuse and had now opened herself up for an interrogation.

"A guy called Craig. I've got to get ready."

"Craig?" Fiona sounded curious. Ready to micromanage her life. "So what kind of work is he in?"

"He works at the auto parts store."

She heard the huff of disapproval in her sister's voice, most likely because Craig didn't have a long university degree, like Peter did. Her sister was married to an engineer.

And then, Gaby jumped as she heard a loud banging noise from outside.

What was it? Her mind caught up as the surge of adrenaline subsided and she realized it was branches, heavy with snow, bumping against the cottage roof. Her landlord hadn't trimmed them back enough in fall. Getting him to do it in winter would be impossible.

Fiona gave a long, obvious sigh. "Can't you move this date?"

"I can't," Gaby replied, annoyed. "I don't want to come to dinner. I'll call you next week, okay?"

Another loud bang made her heart accelerate. She glanced around uneasily, reminding herself it was just the branches.

"But, Gaby –"

Feeling a sense of satisfaction as she cut off her sister's spluttered words, Gaby put the phone down and headed towards the bathroom. Fiona was always so interfering. The micromanaging attitude of her older sister was, most definitely, another reason to make a move.

She went into the bathroom and looked at herself in the mirror, shaking out her long, blond hair. She put on more lipstick – red this time, unlike her toned-down pink she wore for work.

And she would wear a different top tonight. At work they liked her to wear blouses with sleeves. Tonight, she was going to put on her silver spaghetti strap top.

She headed into the tiny bedroom, glad that, although the landlord was bad about property maintenance, the place was fully insulated against the chill. She took off her smart blouse and put on the skimpy, sparkling top.

"Stunning," she told herself, glancing into the full-length mirror.

What about shoes? Her high heeled boots, perhaps? She kicked off the sensible shoes she'd worn for work.

At that moment, the lights flickered, and went out.

"What the hell?" Gaby made a face. Had the power been cut?

Whirling around, she decided to go to the box in the hall, and make sure the switch hadn't tripped, and then call her landlord and give him a piece of her mind. But as she headed there, she heard another loud bang.

That wasn't snow. Adrenaline flooded her as she picked up the difference in the noise.

Had someone broken in? A vagrant, perhaps?

"Who's there?" she shouted, her voice shaking. "Is there anyone there?"

She held her breath in the darkness as she heard the sound of footsteps on the hardwood floor. Terrified, Gaby realized she needed to act. This was like a nightmare made real. Someone had broken in. She needed to call 911 and get the police here, now.

But she'd left her phone in the lounge, after cutting Fiona off. Now it sounded as if this person was already in the lounge.

Then she froze as a voice called out. A man's voice, deep and taunting.

"Where are you hiding? I know you're hiding somewhere nearby! I'll find you this time! I can smell your fear."

Gaby stared at the bedroom door, her heart racing, her breath coming in swift, sharp gasps. This was a nightmare. Not real. Surely, it couldn't be?

He spoke again. "You've left me alone long enough! It's time for me to find you now!"

"No," she whispered.

She had to get away! Whoever this psycho was, she couldn't let him get any closer.

There was a window in the bathroom, leading to the back yard. She could escape through it and run for help.

Her legs were shaking, but she forced herself to overcome the paralysis of fear. She ran into the bathroom, her bare feet slapping on the floor.

"I can hear you!" he taunted.

With desperation giving her wings, she didn't turn to look.

Instead, she yanked the bathroom window open, slamming her hand against the frame to snap the layer of ice. The cold hit her like a fist. Quickly, sobbing with fear, she scrambled through the small gap. It should be too narrow for him to follow. He would have to go around and that would give her time to get away. She hoped.

Her feet plunged down into the soft, icy snow. Far ahead of her, through the flakes, was her landlord's house. If she could reach those bright windows, she would be safe.

Gaby's feet slipped in the drifts. The cold snow burned her unprotected skin. In moments, she couldn't feel her bare feet. But she kept going, gasping as she slid from one snowdrift to another. Spurred on by fear, she fought to reach safety. But it was cold, so cold. The temperature paralyzed her, making her slow. Her limbs felt torpid. Ice flooded her veins.

Behind her, over the blustering wind, she heard him laugh again. She turned to look and there he was, a black shadow in the snow. The snowflakes swirled, disguising his face. All she could see was the dark hood he wore.

Gaby knew she couldn't outrun him. Her legs were numb now and she was shuddering with cold. Her chest had closed up, the air in her lungs freezing.

Feeling disoriented by the cold, she looked up. His black boots were right in front of her face. He pushed her hair back, staring into her eyes. He opened his mouth, and she could feel the heat of his breath on her skin.

"Found you!" he whispered.

She felt the sting of steel as a knife pressed into her throat.

CHAPTER TEN

It was snowing harder outside, Katie saw, as they headed to the home of Elizabeth Martin's parents, who lived in Toronto. She had been the killer's first known victim.

Hopefully Elizabeth Martin's parents might be able to provide a lead, some insight on who their daughter had associated with in the days before she was murdered.

Listening to the rush and rustle of flakes, watching the swish of the wiper blades, Katie felt desperately worried. She feared this snowfall would trigger another kill, and felt helpless to stop it. All she could do was follow evidence and leads, as fast as possible.

"Snow's getting worse," she said quietly to Leblanc, looking out of the car window. "And the wind chill is off the scale. I can't believe it's so cold, and it's only mid-December."

Leblanc sighed. "Winter in Canada. It reminds me how pleasant Paris was, even in a cold snap."

Although she would have loved to know more about working in Paris, Katie knew there wasn't time to ask questions now. Besides, Leblanc didn't like to talk – not to her, anyway.

"We need to look at all possible connections of Elizabeth's. Because a serial killer has to start somewhere, right? She was his first victim. Maybe he knew her, and moved on to strangers."

"I'm not buying that," Leblanc said shortly. "I still believe there's a common thread linking them all that we're missing. My money is on an abusive ex-boyfriend. He could have moved out of the area and his behavior escalated."

"Yes. We need to look at that scenario," she agreed, as abusive exes were always a huge red flag.

"Here we are," Leblanc said.

The house was small and neat, a typical Toronto home, with a manicured lawn and a hanging basket outside the front door.

Katie pulled up in the driveway and they walked quickly to the door.

Mrs. Martin opened the door as soon as they knocked. Her husband stood behind her.

Despite the stress and grief on their faces, both parents were tall and good-looking. Mr. Martin had piercing blue eyes, and Mrs. Martin had golden-blond hair. Their daughter must have been a beauty. Katie felt a surge of pity all over again. Interviewing bereaved relatives was by far the hardest part of her job. These parents looked utterly broken. They had to be devastated.

"Come in, please," Mr. Martin said. He had a weary look on his face, the look of a man who had lost track of time. A man who had been robbed of one of his most important treasures.

"I'm sorry about your daughter," Katie said.

Mrs. Martin pressed her lips tightly together and said nothing. Perhaps she didn't trust the words that might burst from her mouth.

"We need background information," Leblanc said. "Are you able to share something with us? We need to look into Elizabeth's connections, to see if the killer was linked to her in any way."

Mr. Martin sat down opposite and patted the seat next to him, but it was as if Mrs. Martin didn't even see the gesture. She remained standing.

"What have you found out so far?" Mr. Martin asked.

"I'm afraid we don't know much about the case yet, sir," Leblanc answered. "That's why we need this information urgently."

"Her connections, you say?" he asked.

"Yes. Who she was with before she died. Who she spoke to. Anyone she might have had a problem with," Leblanc said.

"I – I'm not sure I know that," Mr. Martin replied.

"When was the last time you saw her?" Leblanc asked.

"Two weeks ago."

"Do you know if she was meeting anyone? If there was anyone new in her life? Anything making her upset or worried?" Katie asked, hoping her suggestions might spark his memories.

"She had recently joined a hiking club."

Katie thought that sounded promising but then Mr. Martin continued, "She was complaining, though, because she had sprained her ankle and hadn't been out with them yet. She was still resting her leg. Even standing on her feet all day in the boutique was difficult, she said."

"Any boyfriends? Any ex-boyfriends?"

The parents exchanged a glance.

"She had a boyfriend last year. I think they broke up at the end of summer. After that, I'm not sure," Mrs. Martin said.

The end of summer felt like a long time ago.

“Was the break-up amicable?” she asked.

“They’d only dated a few months, and I think he started seeing someone else,” Mrs. Martin explained.

“Any problems at work? With neighbors?”

Mrs. Martin shook her head.

Solemnly, Mr. Martin added, “She never had big problems. She was a happy person. She was so talented, so smart. She was going to have such a great life. Our whole family is just devastated."

"I understand."

"It's hard enough to lose a child, especially this way...," Katie thought he was going to break down, but he took a deep breath. "We never know who they will be with when they go out. We don't know what they might do."

“Thank you,” Leblanc said in a kind voice.

Katie exchanged a glance with him. It was time to leave these bereaved parents in peace. There were no more questions she could think of.

But Mr. Martin had said one thing that Katie thought was interesting.

They left, walking out into the swirling flakes.

"What her father said about not knowing who they’re with," Katie said. "I feel that's significant. I think Elizabeth didn’t tell her folks everything happening in her life. They weren’t even sure about her boyfriend. Let's head back to the office and take a look at what we can find, and if Elizabeth was hiding anything from them. Maybe an abusive ex would be something she didn’t want to worry her parents about."

Leblanc raised an eyebrow. “So you’re finally on the same page as me?” he asked in faux-approving tones.

*

Climbing out of the SUV, Katie saw a thick fog hung over the city. Snow drifted steadily around the streetlamps and traffic lights, while on the sidewalk, the yellow cone of light fell on the pure white flakes that drifted on the wind.

The warmth of the police station’s back office felt like a haven after the howling cold of outside.

“We have her call records and messages in the case file,” Leblanc said. “We requested them on the day her body was found, and they arrived this morning.”

"Let's take a look at the call logs and messages first," Katie said. “Do you want to read the messages, and I’ll go through the calls?”

“All right,” Leblanc said, in reluctant tones that told Katie he would rather have had it the other way round.

Katie sat down at the computer and began to go through the call logs.

Most of them seemed to be from her mother and from work. But she was surprised that another number kept popping up.

It was a Toronto number but with a small out-of-town area code. What made it significant was that the calls were all very short. Too short. As if Elizabeth might have been hanging up on the phone on her caller.

“There’s something weird here,” she said.

“There’s something not right here, too.” Leblanc looked up from scanning the messages, his face intent. "These are from the same guy. John. Going back, it looks like they dated a while ago. Then they broke up. And now, these texts are threatening. Let me read them to you."

"It's not over, bitch. We had a good thing going, but you ruined it. There will be payback. You've been warned."

“I thought we were getting back together. But I guess not. Well, if not, you will be sorry."

"I'm going to find you, and when I do, you're going to regret it. Stop hanging up on me. You can’t hide forever. I will find you and then you're in big trouble."

"That doesn't sound like a breakup," Katie said, feeling shocked. She was sure that the out-of-town landline must belong to the writer of these messages, which had been sent from a cell.

“Let me look up the landline quick,” she said, wanting to make sure.

Quickly, she accessed the system and checked the number, nodding in satisfaction.

“It’s registered to a John Reynolds. The same guy, for sure.”

"These are very menacing texts. I think we should go over to this John's place,” Leblanc said.

Katie checked the dates.

The calls and texts had stopped a month ago. She wondered if that had been because John was planning his in-person revenge.

They needed to speak to John urgently, and that meant getting there before the snow shut things down.

She and Leblanc raced out to the car.

CHAPTER ELEVEN

Leblanc climbed into the SUV, firmly taking his place in the driver's seat.

He wished he had one of his team beside him and not this lady agent. He felt as if they had been overridden in the decision to call in the FBI. It had been hotly debated and ultimately, the opinions of him and his team had been ignored. He knew they had the expertise and local knowledge. What did the FBI have? A big, bureaucratic organization, looking to solve a crime that was clearly committed by a local to the area? They were arrogant, and the only way they would be involved was to take over completely.

This investigation could so easily be compromised if it was slowed down. Red tape, bureaucracy and even organizational interests might mean the killer was never found and Leblanc would be powerless to intervene.

Feeling angry and frustrated all over again that such an important case was now in the hands of people who would not understand it, Leblanc started the car. It was about eight miles to John's place, on the outskirts of town. At seven p.m. the traffic was light, but the streets were slick and dangerous with a layer of ice under the fresh snow.

Almost immediately, Leblanc realized it was like driving in a skid pan. Or perhaps in a death trap.

"This is crazy," he complained out loud as the car fishtailed yet again. He felt doubly worried. Worried that the car would actually lose control, and even more concerned that his partner would think he was a terrible driver.

He wasn't! He was an excellent driver. But he was not used to this much ice and snow. He couldn't drive as fast as he needed to.

Sensing impatience emanating from the passenger seat, Leblanc did his best. He pressed the accelerator harder and immediately backed off, gripping the wheel tighter as he felt the car slide again.

"Maybe you should pull over and let me drive," Katie suggested, her tone calm.

"What? Let you drive?" he could hear the incredulity in his own voice.

"I have years of experience. I grew up here." She sounded apologetic, as if she was just trying to help. "I drove every winter for ages. Even before I was legal to drive. It was just how we did things. You haven't been back that long. Things are different in France. Warmer, for a start."

"Two years is more than enough time." Through gritted teeth, Leblanc replied. He couldn't wait to get to John's place. He felt a deep need to prove himself, for the sake of his team who had been so unfairly shot down in the decision making.

"It might be quicker if I drove."

"I don't think so," Leblanc said as he fought to keep the car on the road.

"Pull over," Katie said, and this time, although her tone was still more of a suggestion, the logic finally got through to him. The road was nothing short of a death trap.

"If you must," he said grumpily, easing the car over to the side of the road, reluctance mingling with relief.

Katie climbed into the driver's seat. "I'm not trying to be a hard-ass," she explained. "But this weather is next-level. I'd forgotten how it can be."

Leblanc wasn't going to reply. He had to admit, though, she was damned competent as she sped along the slippery, icy road. The drive was less stressful by far. But the fact she was acing it, where he had failed, was more stressful. By a long way.

They pulled up outside John's place at a quarter past seven. As he climbed out of the car, almost losing his footing on a slick drift, Leblanc took a look at where this abusive ex lived.

At first glance, the place looked like a dump.

The shabby apartment building looked like it might be a converted motel, the kind of place that rented by the hour.

He knocked on the door, waited, and knocked again, harder.

The paint on the door was peeling off in long strips, the window was cracked, and the porch was lined with trash.

It was a grim setting for the type of man who would send threatening texts.

But at least the louder knock had gotten results. In a few seconds, the door was opened.

A tall man with a scruffy goatee stared at them in surprise.

"Are you John Reynolds?" Leblanc asked.

The man shook his head. "I'm his housemate. John's not here. Why do you want him?"

"We want to question him regarding the murder of a previous girlfriend, Elizabeth Martin."

"What?" The man looked at them with wide eyes. There was shock on his face.

"John and Elizabeth broke up a while back, and for a time he was sending her threatening texts." Leblanc said.

"Are you cops?" the man asked cautiously.

"FBI and police, yes," Katie said.

"He's definitely not here." he sounded extremely nervous now.

"When will he be back?" Leblanc prodded.

"Sorry, guys," the man said. "But I really don't know."

"Do you know where he is?"

The man made a thoughtful face. Leblanc was sure he knew. But he wasn't telling.

"It's fine," Katie said soothingly. "We'll come in and wait with you here until he gets back. Do you have a coffee machine?"

Inwardly, Leblanc thought that was a master move. The tall man looked horrified by this proposition.

"He's down at the bar," he admitted. "It's called Costello's, on the street corner. He always goes there after work."

"Description of him?" Katie pressured.

"He's got red hair. A solid looking guy. I think he had a green shirt on this morning."

"Let's head there," Katie said decisively, and they turned back to the car.

The wind was relentless, and the light from the streetlamps was muted and bleak. The snow was coming down hard. Even Katie's knuckles were tight on the steering wheel, he observed, as they made the short trip down the road. They half-stopped, half slid to a halt outside the bar.

Katie led the way inside. They saw John immediately. The red-headed man was seated at the bar, halfway through a glass of beer, talking to a pretty brunette. The bar was warm, filled with the babble of conversation and the smell of malt and hops, ingrained into wood.

Katie headed straight over with Leblanc following closely. As they approached, John looked curiously around.

"FBI and police," Katie introduced them in a low voice. "Can we ask you some questions, Mr. Reynolds?"

Now, John's eyes flew wider. His face changed, looking closed and defensive.

He glanced at the brunette.

“What's this about?” he asked. “I'm socializing. I've got no reason to speak to you."

“Unfortunately, this is very serious. It's regarding the murder of Elizabeth Martin." Katie said, with a tone of threat in the words.

John took another gulp of his beer. Leblanc noted his hands were now shaking.

“I heard about that. I know it was bad. I'm sorry,” he said.

"We know you were sending Elizabeth threatening texts," Leblanc said.

John's face changed. It looked as if someone had punched him in the stomach. He stared at Katie, looking stricken. His hand reached out to grasp the girl's arm.

"Messages?" the brunette asked him accusingly.

"It's - it's nothing, babes. These guys are just looking to rile me. It's an old ex of mine. They're just here to cause trouble," he babbled defensively.

"No," Leblanc said. "We have copies of the texts. They indicate you were angry about the break-up and that you were seeking revenge."

"I wasn't!" John exclaimed angrily. "She was my girlfriend. I was in love with her, and sad when she broke it off."

"You should have left her alone," the brunette said.

"Seriously, I am not a murderer!" he snapped.

"Where were you last Sunday night? Did you go anywhere near her place?" Leblanc probed. Elizabeth had been reported missing on the Monday, he recalled, when she hadn't arrived at work.

“Sunday? I was at work all day. Saturday, too.”

"Work?"

“I'm a ski instructor. Weekends are my busiest time for work. With this cold snap, the season's been pumping.”

"You didn't take time off?"

"No! I didn't kill her! I wouldn't have done that. I worked the late shift on both days, from midday to eight p.m.”

"And then?"

John pressed his lips together. He didn't want to say. "I didn't do this," he repeated.

"Unless you tell us your whereabouts, we are going to arrest you on suspicion," Katie threatened.

Leblanc thought John looked scared.

"I did not contact Elizabeth for a month," John said. "She blocked me. She blocked my number. I had no way to get in touch with her."

So that's why the messages had stopped, Leblanc realized.

"What were you doing on Sunday night?"

John sighed. "I was – I was with a client at the ski lodge," he said, as the brunette turned to him furiously. "Sometimes – well, we're not supposed to, but sometimes clients get friendly, and it ends up being part of the service," he said, as the brunette turned to him furiously.

"Can you confirm this?"

The brunette banged her glass down on the table. She scooted off her stool and stormed out of the bar.

"Now look what you've done!" John said in appalled tones.

"Mr. Reynolds. Your whereabouts?" Leblanc pressured.

He sighed.

"I was with her Saturday and Sunday night. I'll show you the texts. And we had dinner Saturday night at the lodge. I paid. I can show you the credit card slip, and you can confirm with her. She lives in Peterborough and her name's Madeline."

"Give us the details," Katie insisted.

As John scrolled through his phone, showing the texts and the timeline, Leblanc felt a sense of disappointment. It appeared this strong suspect had an alibi and was not Elizabeth's killer.

Their lead had fizzled out. It was after eight now, snowing heavily, and they were out of time. With a sense of doom, Leblanc realized there was no other angle they could explore tonight. The killer was still far ahead, and this snowy night would allow him to strike again.

CHAPTER TWELVE

Katie felt as if all their efforts so far had been proving futile. How could they fight back against this monster, when the weather was taking his side tonight and shutting everything down?

"By tomorrow, we're going to have a third victim. I'm sure of it," she said, feeling frustrated and sad, as they headed out of the bar and into the freezing darkness.

Leblanc nodded. He opened his phone and pressed some keys.

"Closest motel is a mile down the road. I think we should check in there. It'll be easier than heading back in this storm."

"Let's do that," Katie agreed.

She drove the short distance, bumping and sliding over the snowy ground, feeling a sense of relief when they reached the motel. It looked old and basic, but the windows were brightly lit and she hoped it would be warm.

She parked outside and they climbed out, staggering as the wind hit them like a fist. Leblanc held the door open for her, hanging onto it with all his might as the wind threatened to rip it away.

Inside, the receptionist looked excited to see two guests arriving so late, and in a storm.

"Welcome, welcome! Isn't this cold unseasonal? Such an early snap. Only the middle of December, and already there's snow enough for the whole of winter! Brrrr! We can give you two rooms on the second floor. You'll find extra blankets in the closet. Help yourselves to anything you need in the kitchenette. We have wi-fi and there are several fast-food places that deliver, or there's a small eatery on the next block."

Katie felt grateful for her friendliness. At this stage, she felt she needed her faith to be restored in humanity. She felt too tired to eat, but gratefully accepted a couple of bottles of water, before heading upstairs to her room.

As she unlocked the small, carpeted room, she realized that she would be spending the night on the borders of the lake where her childhood home was. Her old home was on the other side of Lake

Ontario, perhaps twenty-five miles from here as the crow flew, or the speedboat sailed.

Shivering as she looked out of the window, Katie saw her room actually had a view of the lake's frozen expanse. On the other side, lay all her memories.

She thought again about Josie. How brave she'd been, how adventurous. Always the daredevil out of the two of them. How they had laughed together. Agony twisted inside her as she wondered what had happened to her twin.

She could visit her parents while she was here. The thought occurred to Katie with shocking suddenness. Just as quickly, she decided against it. She was not ready to see them again. It would bring trouble into her life all over again. They still blamed her for Josie's disappearance, Katie knew. That was okay. She blamed herself, too.

Feeling suddenly lonely and wanting a friendly voice, Katie decided instead to call her mentor.

Ex-FBI agent Timms, today a criminal law consultant, had supported Katie when she'd first joined the Bureau. He'd felt more like a father figure to her than her real father had been. He was a stocky guy with piercing green eyes and a no-nonsense attitude.

Timms answered on the first ring.

"Winter," he said. "Good to hear you. I believe you're up in Canada with a special task force?"

"We're tracking a suspected serial killer," she admitted. "But we're getting nowhere."

"Why's that?" he asked. "Do you have time to discuss it?"

Grateful that he'd offered, especially since focusing on a case always helped her personal issues to fade into the background, she explained. "I need a different perspective. I'm hitting a brick wall, and I feel like we're running out of time."

"I know this must be hard for you," he said. "The serial killer cases are the toughest ones to crack. There is no motive, just random bloody mayhem. But you need to be patient, and scrutinize all the evidence carefully, because he will make a mistake."

"I know, but it is ripping me apart that by the time he's made it, another woman will be dead."

"They're evil people," Timms agreed. "And often, frighteningly intelligent, too. You need to get in his mind. Is he hitting a certain profile in his victims? Is there a common thread?"

"They're all the same type. Young, slim, blonde, good looking."

"Could he have dated more than one of them in the past?" he asked.

"It doesn't seem so, although we are still exploring any possible connection. As far as we can tell, they don't know each other. We're not sure how he finds them."

Timms was silent for a while and Katie knew he was thinking carefully about what she had said.

"Maybe you don't need to think about how he finds them. Maybe you need to think about why he finds them," he said eventually.

To Katie, the room suddenly seemed brighter. Timms had reminded her that she needed to use the talent and instincts she had for placing herself in a killer's shoes. She'd cracked three seemingly impossible cases during her career by focusing on the killer's thought processes, which had given her an insight into who he was. She hadn't done this enough in this case, she realized. And it was important.

"That's so helpful. You've grounded me again," she admitted.

"I'm glad to have been of help. Stay safe out there. Call me any time if you need me."

"I'll be in touch again soon," she promised.

They hung up. Katie showered quickly, glad that the water was steaming hot. And the bed was warm, she thought, climbing inside.

Was it possible to find the killer by thinking the way he did? And was she ready to explore such an evil mind? With so much to think about, Katie didn't know if she would manage to sleep, but when she did, she plunged into a nightmare she hadn't had for years.

The first sound she heard was Josie. She was screaming.

Katie ran to find her twin. She burst out onto the lakeshore. There was Josie. Somehow she'd fallen on the ice and was sliding away from the shore. Their father was standing on the dock, watching, with a smile on his face.

"Daddy!" Katie wailed. "Come help!"

He didn't move.

"Daddy!" she yelled.

Suddenly he was gone. He'd never been there at all, she realized with a wrench. She had been the one who should have helped, but now it was too late.

Josie was being dragged into the darkness by a shadowy figure she could not see. It was like a nightmare, as if time had moved faster than real time.

She felt dizzy and sick, as she watched her sister being pulled away. She cried out, running after her. Too late. Too late.

Katie ran onto the ice. She was afraid, but there was no choice. Josie was being taken, but she was also trying to save herself. Katie reached her, grabbed her hand and felt it slip away. She was going to lose her.

The next sound was Katie's own voice. She was screaming too.

Katie woke up shouting, panic surging through her. It was a minute before she realized where she was. Shivering, she sat up in the bed, pulling the covers around her. Her heart was pounding. She could still hear Josie's screams.

"No," she said out loud. "No."

She forced herself to breathe deeply. The dream had been so powerful, so strong.

She was sweating and shaking, feeling sick and hollow inside. She looked out the window to see snow still falling heavily outside.

And then her phone rang.

Katie grabbed it, surprised that it was already seven a.m.

It was Detective Clark on the line.

"There's been another murder," he said, his voice heavy. "A walker just found a woman's body, on the shores of the lake, on the US side, near Watertown. You need to get to the scene as soon as possible."

CHAPTER THIRTEEN

Katie rushed out of her motel room, meeting Leblanc in the motel's lobby. He looked stressed, and his shirt was crumpled, as if he'd gotten dressed as quickly as she had once he'd heard the news.

" Any breakfast?" the receptionist sang cheerily, but Katie barely heard the words. She felt angry beyond belief that this man had killed again. A coward, dumping the body under cover of snow. Another life lost and they were no closer to catching him.

"It'll take an hour to get to the scene," Leblanc said. "You drive."

They headed out of the motel. Climbing inside the car, Katie saw that the storm had eased and the streets had been plowed. Even so, she was seething and could barely concentrate on the road.

How had this been allowed to happen again? Even though she'd suspected he would strike in the next big snowfall, she felt so helpless. While she'd been asleep, a murder had occurred. Surely, somehow, she could have prevented it?

"You don't have to speed," Leblanc said, sounding more nervous than she'd ever heard him. "The police will be there already."

Katie drove on, taking the right turn that led them over the bridge. She kept her eyes on the road, but her mind was elsewhere. In her dream, she'd been on the ice as well. Had she relived her sister's fate through the killer's eyes? She shivered at the thought.

"You okay?" Leblanc asked, sounding worried.

"I'll be fine," she said. They drove in silence, until he spoke again.

"At least the police got to the scene quickly because the local patrols were keeping an eye out. So there might be something there to help us."

"The local patrols didn't see him dumping her," Katie responded, feeling exasperated. "That means he's doing it at night."

The road led them alongside the lake. Gazing at it, remembering her dream, Katie was starting to hate the frozen wasteland of water all over again.

*

When they reached the US side, she saw the police had set up a roadblock and closed the highway. The taillights stretched for miles, but she turned on the siren and light, and raced along in the emergency lane, grateful that the snowplow had been through.

She pulled up at the roadblock feeling stressed. A police officer from the Watertown PD, who was stationed at the roadblock, directed her.

"It's about half a mile on," he said. "The walker who found the body was able to call a passing patrol and they were on the scene almost immediately."

"Have you gotten a positive ID?" Katie asked him.

"Not yet, but the woman is young, in her twenties. She's blond, wearing a silver top and black pants."

By the time they arrived at the scene, the official vehicles were all there. Katie parked, and she and Leblanc ran toward the lake, where a tent had been set up. The sky was a brilliant clear, but apart from the tracks left by the police, Katie could see nothing but white.

Detective Clark met them at the scene. He looked stressed, and as if he'd also had a bad night's rest.

"Come this way," he said. "The body is still lying where it was found."

Wondering if this scene would provide any clues, Katie rushed behind him, slipping and slithering over the drifts of snow until they reached the trodden path to the lake.

"It's the same MO," Clark said. "Same place, same time of day. Same body position and again, there's no ID on her."

"Was she killed here?" Katie asked, trying to picture how this had happened.

"Coroner says the ritualistic stabbings are the same but his guess is that exposure was probably the main contributing factor to her death. There's no sign that she was dragged. He might have carried her."

She felt utter revulsion at the idea that the killer had brought another dead woman here, on the ice, to lie out in the open, in the cold. He was making a statement to the world. Gleefully displaying the bodies while hiding away like a coward.

"There are some tracks nearby from snowmobiles. More than one, crisscrossed near the scene. They're very faint, but at least they're visible."

"Despite the storm?" Leblanc asked, surprised.

“They were protected from the worst of the snow by an overhanging bank. We’ll photograph them in case that’s how he brought her out there,” Clark said.

"Where is she?" Katie said.

"Out there on the ice. But don't go there!" Now Clark's voice held a note of alarm. “It could be dangerous."

"I'll be okay."

Katie knew from spending an entire childhood on this frozen lake, what the moods and nuances of the ice were. She was used to stepping carefully over it, sensing its thickness, waiting to feel if any cracks were forming under her feet.

She stepped out and began walking to the scene, some fifty yards away, trying to think as the killer might have done while he traversed this risky route.

Reaching the scene, Katie saw that the body had been carefully laid out on the snow, which was faintly stained with crimson. The woman's face was turned toward them, but her eyes were open. Katie could see that she had been pretty, with a clear complexion, regular features and a full mouth, which was slightly open. She lay with her mouth open. Inside, frozen to her tongue, Katie could see the wooden figure of a bishop.

It was difficult to take in the stark reality of this death. Katie stared, her eyes narrowed, trying to think calmly and suppress her emotions.

Then, finally, she nodded. This scene was confirming what she had suspected. The killer was not targeting his victims because of who they were. But rather, who they represented. Searching for a common thread between them was no longer important. The common thread was in their looks, their build, what they meant to him.

He was targeting young, slim, pretty blondes because they were somebody else in his mind. Hence the ritualistic presentation of the bodies.

Why, she wondered helplessly. What did the chess pieces mean and what were their significance to him?

But as she turned away, she realized another important piece of information.

The killer had walked out on this lake, at night. Just like she had done, but in the dark. He'd been carrying a body. And he had gone far out, almost to the place where the ice became dangerous.

She turned back.

"I know something about him," she called as she picked her way to shore. Clark had come halfway out to meet her, looking worried.

"You know something about him?" Clark asked, sounding incredulous.

"He must be familiar with the ice. As familiar as I am. He understands it. He's someone who knows this lake. Who can tell if the ice will hold."

The killer was a man who knew the lake. A man who had been there many times before.

"That must be how he's crossing the border. By traversing the lake," Clark agreed. "Either by speedboat, or else on foot. Maybe even on a snowmobile if the ice is thick enough. That would be why our border checks and roadblocks have picked nothing up so far."

A shout came from behind them.

"We have an ID on the victim. Her landlord just called in," one of the police shouted. "Her name is Gaby Mackay and she lives in a place just outside Watertown. Her landlord said there are signs of a struggle in the snow. Apparently there are some visible footprints. They were sheltered by an overhanging tree."

This was the moment they'd been waiting for. He had made his first mistake and by doing so, revealed some personal information they could use to find him. Feeling determined to capitalize on it, Katie hurried back to shore, treading over the shifting, slippery ice as fast as she dared.

CHAPTER FOURTEEN

Leblanc felt hopeful as he turned away and climbed into the SUV. This time, he opted for the passenger side, because some things just weren't worth fighting over, and it was better to use common sense.

But he felt buoyed that there was evidence, finally. The killer had been careless at last.

Getting in behind the wheel, Katie looked equally determined. Her sheer grit and dedication was surprising to Leblanc. From his experience so far with the FBI, he had expected her to be more arrogant.

"Let's go see what he left for us," she said.

The cottage wasn't far away. Katie drove purposefully up the snowy track and onto the road, where she accelerated to a speed that had Leblanc discreetly digging his nails into his palms.

It was not that he distrusted her driving. He respected her ability to maneuver in these conditions. But he could not help feeling a serious adrenaline rush as she accelerated up to the icy bend at the same speed a competitive cross-country skier might have flung themselves down a slope.

They flew down the main street and then turned onto a narrow country track, which had been plowed, with the snow piled high on either side.

He took a deep breath as she swung the wheel around the icy curve.

"Did you drive like this when you were young?" he asked.

Katie was too intently focused on the road to take her eyes off it, but she nodded.

"I started driving when I was thirteen. My dad let me, as long as he was with me, because there was nobody around most of the time and he thought we should know how. It was very quiet out there on the back roads. But my first time didn't go so well. I nearly drove off the road and got stuck in a snow bank. Josie, my twin, was always the better driver."

Leblanc wanted to ask her about her twin but there was something in Katie's face that told him this might be a sensitive topic.

Katie did not slow down until she reached the little cottage beyond the main farmhouse. As soon as she stopped beside the three police cars from the Watertown precinct, she was out and running, with Leblanc right behind her.

They rushed past the cottage and headed straight to the knot of policemen in the backyard.

“We’re from the task force,” Leblanc introduced himself breathlessly. “This is where the victim lived? And you say there are tracks here?

"Yes. They were sheltered by that tree. The branches must have protected them from the storm,” the closest detective explained.

Leblanc stooped down and took a look. He felt a thrill of horror imagining the scene that had played out. The small footsteps, bare in the snow. Every toe defined. He glanced at the window. She’d scrambled out and run, but she hadn’t gotten far. Barefoot in that cold, and wearing that skimpy top, she would have been overpowered by the chill in a minute.

Then, the heavy tracks of boots showed that the killer had run in pursuit.

"Let's go in through the front door," Katie said. "It will give us a chance to see things the way the killer saw them. We can think the way he did, then."

Leblanc nodded.

Walking around, he saw the wooden front door was splintered. He’d broken in, smashed the flimsy latch, and gone to grab her.

“The lights are off,” Katie observed. “He might have tripped the main box. It’s here, by the front door.”

Leblanc paced through the small, overly warm cottage, uneasily imagining this psycho doing the same thing in the dark. He looked at the window. Gaby Mackay had tried her best to escape. She’d done the only thing she could do, but in the end, the cold had been the killer’s friend.

Through the window, they stared at the portion of tracks that were visible.

Katie pointed to the last footprint.

“You can see she was slowing down. It was too cold for her. Just too cold,” she said sadly. “She wasn't dressed for it. This cottage is like a furnace. She had no chance outside."

They turned and walked back out of the cottage. At the door, they met Clark, who was bustling back from the scene, looking motivated.

"We can guess at his height and build and the approximate weight from the prints. The techs will need to confirm it, but those shoes are a size eleven, with a heavy, distinctive tread. So our killer is tall. He's a big, tall man. Probably at least six foot. Not fat, but strong."

"That narrows it down, somewhat," Katie agreed thoughtfully.

A thought occurred to Leblanc.

"How was she found?" he wondered. "And when was she found?"

"The landlord has already given a statement to police. He's over here." Grant pointed to a stressed-looking man in a heavy overcoat, standing beyond the cottage's small wooden fence.

Leblanc headed over to speak to him.

"When did you notice that your tenant was missing? Were you the one who called it in?" he asked.

The man nodded. "Gaby was supposed to meet a boyfriend at a bar in town. She never arrived, and wasn't answering her phone, so he got worried. He came out here and found her place open, and saw she was missing. He walked to the main house to see if she was there. When I saw she was gone, we phoned in a missing person report immediately."

"When was this?" Katie asked, sounding suddenly suspicious.

"Must have been around half past eight last night. We didn't see the footprints then. It was snowing heavily and we didn't notice that placc under the tree where they were protected."

Leblanc felt annoyed beyond belief, and glancing at Katie, he saw she shared his sentiments completely.

If the local Watertown police had been wider awake, they could have called this through to the task force immediately. Starting the hunt last night could even have allowed them to find this woman before she was killed.

"Why didn't you tell us?" he turned to the local detective.

"There was no reason to," the man shot back.

"Your slowness cost this woman her life!" he snapped

The detective stared back at him, defensive and arrogant.

"We didn't know it was a crime scene. We had nothing to go on. We didn't know what we were looking for, except that she was missing. How many young womcn run away? We didn't know anything!"

"Run away in the middle of a cold snap, leaving the front door open?" Leblanc said.

"Besides, you warned us off investigating," another detective added, overhearing the conversation as he walked by.

"What? How?" Leblanc couldn't believe this. At such a critical time, petty politics were in play?

"Well, those first two bodies were found on American soil but the whole investigation was taken over by the Toronto police. Now the FBI is involved. Too little, too late, I think. All I'm saying is that if we'd been kept in the loop, we would have known better."

Leblanc didn't believe a word. "We sent a clear update out to all local precincts. Are you deaf or blind?"

The man drew himself up angrily. Before he could reply, Leblanc continued.

"From now on, consider yourselves in the loop. And if you hear of any woman missing, or attacked, or grabbed – we need to know. As a matter of urgency."

Unable to speak further without yelling, he stomped away.

"Hey!" One of the detectives called after him. "We know our job! We're just following protocols!"

Leblanc knew that it was hopeless to expect cooperation from these men. The killer had been running loose in their area, and they had done nothing to stop him. Their arrogance, resentment, and small-town attitude had all combined at the worst possible moment.

"These guys need a serious shake-up," Katie muttered to him.

Leblanc was glad she felt the same. The locals had let them down. Whether through genuine ignorance or ruffled feathers, they had allowed the killer to slip through the net and now he was gone.

The detective in charge was arrogant and defensive. Now he could see that even the young police officers present at the scene were clearly inexperienced.

Leblanc couldn't risk saying anything more in their criticism. Getting angrier wouldn't help.

He'd just have to hope that the killer didn't choose to strike in the Watertown area again.

He turned away, conversing in a low voice with Katie and Clark, who looked just as annoyed.

"We're getting nowhere," she said. "We know a little more about the victims' connections, but the killer is too smart for us. The local police are unwilling to help us, and we can't rely on them. Not unless we have to, which we might," she sighed.

"What's our next move?" he asked.

"We need to try and forget about this setback, and focus on the killer. I need to get into his head," she explained.

"I think we're all done with the victims' connections," Leblanc surprised himself by agreeing with her. "

“The other two members of the task force, Chris Johnson and Detective Damien Anderson, are going to take a look at camera footage on the street corner near the clinic and see what they can find,” Clark said.

“We need to look at the killer himself,” Katie decided. “We know more about him now. We know he's familiar with the ice. Unafraid of it. And that he must have lived close to the lake for a while, or probably still does."

Leblanc nodded. "We know something about his build, his size. He's tall. He can lift and carry a body with ease."

"He's physically fit. He's a survivor," she said. "He must be a younger man. Definitely not elderly. I am sure he is killing because of the way these women look. He is killing because of their hair color, because of their eyes, because of their body type. He loves them but yet he hates them."

"In his twenties? His thirties?" Guessing like that could be dangerous, Leblanc knew, but they had to narrow down a picture of him.

Katie grimaced. “Definitely younger. Twenties or thirties. I think I’m leaning toward that age category because why would he have waited till his forties before starting a spree of such violent murders?”

“And his occupation? He’s a clever man.”

"Yes. He is. But I feel he’s more likely a fisherman, or a hunter," Katie suggested.

"Why?"

She sighed. "He knows the outdoors. He’s mobile. His time seems to be his own. And he has knife skills and knows how to work with his hands. How to use a blade."

She didn't have to spell out the obvious. The killer had the hands of a carpenter or a craftsman.

"Could he have made those chess pieces?" Leblanc recalled they looked crude and rough.

"He could havc. I also thought they looked handmade,” Katie agreed.

“Why would he make them? Why not buy them? What does that say about him?”

“It might mean they’re very important to him personally. That these chess pieces are linked to the motivation for these murders.”

“How would that be?” Leblanc puzzled.

“That’s where it gets complex. There are many possible reasons and we need to keep theorizing. But for now, at least we know they are all from the same set, and he must be keeping it somewhere. It will provide evidence, if we find it."

So now, they had some pieces of the puzzle, even if they all didn’t fit yet. The killer was a man who knew the ice. He was probably a hunter or a fisherman, or someone who worked on the ice. Someone who knew the lake, and its moods.

“We need to chase him,” Leblanc said. “Let’s go question the locals. We should start with the hunters and fishermen in this section of the lake.”

"It’s a huge shoreline. We should comb different areas, to cover as much ground as we can. And stay in touch with each other so we know where we’re at,” Katie agreed.

Leblanc knew had to be careful not to stereotype the killer, but it would be a good move to look at all the hunters and fishermen in the area. Even if he wasn’t one of them, they could well have seen something.

They would find the source of the chess pieces, Leblanc promised himself, filled with anger as he remembered those running footprints. This now felt personal. They would find him, whatever it took.

CHAPTER FIFTEEN

Katie climbed into the SUV, realizing that this was the first time on the case she'd been operating solo, without Leblanc. Perhaps it would be better that way, she thought. She might make faster progress without the Gallic arrogance seething from the seat next door.

Although, she had to admit, he was intelligent and perceptive. Just a shame about his attitude. Even so, on this case, she knew she had to trust him. She had to trust his instincts and his ability to read people.

Katie hoped that they would achieve better harmony and that they would be able to work together, in the end. But for now, she was happy to be on her own.

The two most recent bodies had been found on the southern shore of the lake, about ten miles apart. Ten miles was a long way and Katie felt briefly discouraged as she thought of the multitudes of cabins, chalets, and shacks that the area would hold. The hunters and fishermen and visitors. The people who lived off grid and in the fringes of society.

She thought that this ten mile radius was significant and that the killer might have started dumping the bodies in what was his home territory. That would make sense, because as awareness of his crimes spread, he would find it riskier to cover a wider area. That meant he was more likely to be a US national who had ventured onto Canadian soil to commit murder, than the other way round.

Katie knew these shores well and she was familiar with the places she'd known when she lived here. That had been more than ten years ago, but she had the feeling things didn't change fast in this part of the world.

Places came back to her as memories surged.

Right on the edge of the town, she remembered, and a short distance from the lake, there was a campsite with an old fish and chip shop nearby.

And there was another site nearby, which was on a rough, narrow road. It was busier in the winter. It was located near a tiny general store, with some bait and tackle, and fishing and camping equipment, and a little café which mostly served hot food to ice fishers.

That would be the best place to start.

Katie didn't need to put the coordinates into her GPS. She knew how to get there from memory.

She set off, the SUV skimming along the snowplowed road, hoping that most of the fishermen would not yet be out on the ice. She hoped she could reach them when they were still arriving at the site, or holed up in their huts.

She was surprised how long-forgotten details came back to her as she drove. She remembered that particular tree by the roadside. Half of it had been struck by lightning, but half still grew, giving it an odd-shaped look that hadn't changed much in a decade.

Just beyond the tree was the turnoff to the fishing site.

She was right. It didn't look to have changed at all. Possibly there were a couple more of the small cabins, but that was it. It was peaceful, calm, and freezing cold.

Katie parked on the side of the road, and then walked along the shore, on a trail that led to the closest fishing hut

She could see the fishing huts more closely now. She'd been right about the timing, she realized. Men were getting ready for the day, with the tackle put out on the ice, near the shore. Some were already venturing outside. They were wearing bulky clothes and had wrapped scarves around their heads. Some were wearing sunglasses. Others had plastic goggles over their eyes to protect from the icy gusts of wind that still flurried.

When Katie had been very young, she'd thought the tents and huts to be romantic and adventurous. She'd dreamed of overnighting in one of them.

But as she'd gotten older, she had understood how difficult it could be to camp out near the lake or on the ice. It was usually freezing cold, was almost certainly uncomfortable, and could be very risky.

If they didn't have bed frames, the fishermen had to use thick foam sleeping mats on the floor to insulate them from the icy ground.

In winter, this was a stark and self-contained world.

As she reached the closest hut, the door opened and a man stepped out, carrying an auger. She recognized this long, cylindrical tool with a sharp blade on the end as being a common and necessary piece of equipment for cutting through the ice. But now, Katie found she was looking at that tool suspiciously, wondering if the killer had used a similar weapon in his stabbings.

He stared at her curiously as she picked her way toward him.

"Morning," she said. "I'm Agent Winter from the FBI. We are tracking a suspect in a recent murder that occurred near here."

"A suspect?" the man asked, cocking his head to one side. "What are you hoping to find?"

Katie saw immediately that this man didn't match up to the brief they had for the killer's description. He was shorter, maybe five-six, and she guessed his shoe size might be an eight.

"We're hoping to get information on the killer. He has dumped his victims out on the lake," Katie explained.

The fisherman thought a minute and then nodded. "A friend was telling me yesterday about a girl's body, dumped in the ice a few miles down. Is that something to do with this?"

Katie nodded. "That's correct. There was another body dumped last night."

"Another one?" the man asked in consternation.

"We think the killer might be part of the fishing or hunting community. He seems to know this section of the lake very well. So we're asking around, hoping that someone might know something that could help us."

"I only heard about it yesterday. I don't know anything about it. I wish I could help you, though." The fisherman pulled his scarf tighter around his neck. "Having dead bodies turning up will give this place a bad reputation."

"I hear you," Katie said.

"It's tough enough to make a living here," he said, "with the season being so short. We don't need that kind of thing." He sighed. "A man wants to feel safe, at night. Not like there's a killer out there causing trouble."

"Have you heard of any trouble?" Katie asked.

"No," he shook his head. "I've been here a week, camping out, and I haven't heard anything at night. No commotion, no shouting. No vehicles, even. But then, I do keep to myself."

"Do you know any of the people in this area who play chess? Or who like to carve figurines out of wood?" Katie said. "That could point us in the right direction."

The man shook his head. "Nobody comes to mind," he said. "But I'm sure there's a lot I don't know about the folk nearby. We don't talk much, and when we do, it's about the weather, the fish. The things that affect our lives."

“Thanks for the information,” Katie said. “Could you point me to someone who might know more?”

"Those guys over there, they might know something. They're brothers, and their father owns the general store near here."

He pointed to two more fishermen, swathed in furs, who were about to head out onto the lake.

Katie hurried over to them.

"I'm FBI Agent Winter,” she said. “Do you have a minute to talk to me?”

The two brothers turned from organizing their tackle. They looked as surprised as the other fisherman had.

“What’s this about?” the closer one asked. He didn’t sound friendly and in fact seemed defensive.

“We’re investigating a murder," she said. "There's a serial killer who is dumping his victims in the lake. You’ve probably heard about it. I'm wondering if any of you have seen anything suspicious. It could be a local involved."

They both nodded as if putting two and two together. But their attitude didn’t warm.

Katie noted that they looked very similar, and were both bearded. However, they couldn’t be more than five-seven or five-eight in height.

The closer brother looked at her with suspicion. “None of the guys in our area are killers," he said.

“Has anyone been behaving unusually? Coming or going late at night?”

“No, ma’am. Nothing like that,” the closer man emphasized.

Katie had a feeling that in this close-knit community, they would trust and protect each other rather than spill the beans to a random law enforcement agent. She remembered from when she was younger that people preferred to live by their own rules in this remote and freezing place.

“I believe your father owns the general store,” she said. “Is he here today?”

The two men looked at each other and seemed to reach a decision. "

“Yes. He’s in. The store’s up there, at the top of that track. Go talk to him," said the first.

Light dawned. They were being helpful because they wanted her not to talk to them anymore.

Katie turned away and headed to the store.

A small pickup truck was parked outside. A man was offloading a bag from the trunk. He looked about sixty years old, swathed in winter gear. Katie thought, as he turned and smiled at her, that he seemed friendlier than his sons. Or perhaps he thought she was a potential customer.

“FBI. I'm investigating a murder," she said. “Your sons said I should come talk to you.”

He nodded. "It's terrible. Terrible. I heard all about it on the news last night, and of course it's got everyone talking."

"I know this is a small community. Perhaps someone knows something?” Katie prodded him. “Is there anyone who has been acting suspiciously or unusually in the last week or two? Who has been coming and going at night?"

The store owner thought for a minute, rubbing his hand over his beard.

“We’re all peace-loving folk here. I would say if there’s anyone who could have done such a thing, it’s Zack. But he’s been the way he is for a long time, though.”

"What are you talking about?" Katie asked, feeling hopeful.

"Zack lives about a mile to the north, near the forest. Off the grid. Everyone who knows him, knows to keep away from him.”

"Why is that?" Katie asked, feeling eager to know.

"He's an ex-veteran. He served in the Army but got kicked out. He has PTSD and is a bit of a loner. He chases others out of his 'territory,' as he calls it. He's threatened people with a knife in the past. I wouldn't advise you go and see him alone, lady."

The mention of a knife had all her instincts prickling.

"Can you show me where he stays?" she asked. "I need to speak to Zack urgently."

CHAPTER SIXTEEN

Leblanc climbed into his car and set off, feeling relieved to be working separately from Katie. He'd have a chance to explore his own theories. With luck, if he could solve the case, it might mean the end of this FBI interference. They didn't need it, he thought.

He had a clear plan for where he wanted to go. The most recent victim, Gaby, had worked in a doctor's office. It was possible, Leblanc decided, that they had ice fishermen on their books. That would narrow down the field of suspects. It would be far more logical to approach it this way, he decided, than going from person to person on the lake's massive shoreline.

He hoped he would prove to Katie that a methodical approach, and focusing on the suspect's contacts, was the way forward in solving this crime.

During the short drive, Leblanc decided on his strategy. He would ascertain what patients the clinic had treated, where they were from, how recently they had been in the clinic, and whether they had shown any interest in Gaby.

He pulled up outside the clinic feeling positive.

Through the glass windows, he noticed the clinic's interior seemed brightly lit and welcoming. It was very easy to stand here and to see what a bystander might have seen. It was almost like a movie screen, looking through the big glass window.

Certainly, it would have been very easy for the killer to have tracked Gaby's movements. He would have seen exactly when she left.

He imagined this psychopath watching as she headed out of the clinic, knowing her timing, making his plans. Perhaps he'd followed her at a distance and waited for her to get comfortable in her cottage before he struck.

It was a chilling thought and again, anger surged inside him that the guy had gotten away with this.

Not again, he promised himself.

Walking into the clinic, immediately he sensed the atmosphere. It was quiet, stressed, tense. A redheaded woman was seated in reception. She must be a temp, he guessed, standing in today after Gaby's death.

She couldn't feel too good about taking her place after a colleague had been tracked to her home and murdered, he guessed, with a flash of sympathy.

"Detective Leblanc," he introduced himself. "I'm here following up on the murder."

"It's so tragic. It's just unreal. Gaby is not here anymore. None of us can believe it," the redhead explained.

"We think she may have been killed by someone with local knowledge. In particular, any of the local hunters and fishermen. Do you recall any of them coming in for treatment in the past week or two?"

"I know we have a few on our books. I'll get you the names of people who have been here in the past two weeks, but I'll have to check with the manager first, and then print them out from her office."

"Please, go ahead. I'll wait," Leblanc hoped his presence in the office would hurry this process up.

There was a couch in reception. Leblanc sat with a sigh. He hoped this wasn't a waste of time and that they would be able to provide a list of patients.

He felt impatient and also competitive as he sat there, twiddling his fingers while Katie might be making better progress on her side.

Even Leblanc sometimes rolled his eyes at how competitive he was. Passionate, as he preferred to think of it. He had been passionate about his job on the streets of Paris, and he was equally passionate in this snowy cold, even though he sometimes wondered about the sanity of his decision to stay here.

He'd come back two years ago after his mother had been diagnosed with cancer. He'd spent six months living with her and looking after her, working in the local Quebec unit. When she had finally passed, he hadn't felt ready to go back to Paris, and the Toronto police commissioner had offered him a job. He'd decided to take it for a while, and today, here he was still.

He turned back to the receptionist, who had returned from the office and was working diligently on her computer.

"Have you obtained the list of patients?" he asked.

"Yes. I'm just waiting for it to print," she said.

At that moment, to his relief, the printer started humming and one page spilled out.

Only one page, with a very short list of four names.

"We do have a number of hunters and ice fishermen on our books, but we haven't had many of them in here in the past two weeks. These are the ones who've been in. We can't give you any other information except that they made an appointment, due to patient confidentiality."

"I understand," Leblanc said.

At that moment, one of the nurses rushed in. She headed directly over to Leblanc. She looked stressed, and she glanced behind her before speaking.

"I overheard you from the other room," she said to Leblanc in a quiet voice. "I know you want to follow up on the list of patients, but there is someone else you might want to speak to also. Someone who has been a problem with Gaby in the past, so much so that when he made his last appointment, we didn't allow him to speak to her. We sent someone else out to deal with him. That was about three weeks ago but it might still be important, don't you think?" She stared at him anxiously.

"Yes. It could be very important." Leblanc felt hugely thankful that she'd overheard. This information could provide a valuable break in the case. "Who is he? What happened?" Leblanc asked.

"He's a patient who lives locally. I know he has a cabin near the lake, and is off the grid. And the past couple of times he was here, he behaved very inappropriately around her."

"In what way?"

"Harassing her. Asking her for dates. He mentioned her hair. In fact, he seemed obsessed with her hair. Said he loves blondes. He actually used to try to reach over, touch her hair, stroke it."

"Is that so?" Leblanc was feeling more and more positive about this new lead.

"His name is Kyle Davis."

"How tall is he?" Leblanc asked, wanting to check if this man fell within the physical parameters they had identified.

"About six feet. And around thirty years old. He is very strong looking. I don't know if he's a hunter or a fisherman, but he definitely looks like that type of person."

The physical description was within the parameters. He nodded as the nurse continued.

"I used to think he was harmless, but now that I know what people can do, I'm scared. I'm wondering if all of us ignored a big potential problem in him. I think now that he might be dangerous and obsessive." She sounded very worried and stared at Leblanc appealingly.

“I’m going to head there straight away. Do you know where he lives? What's his address?" Leblanc asked.

“It’s all the way down by the lake. Seventeen Lakeside Drive, I think. He has a cabin there on a small plot of land. I remember he was telling Gaby once she must come and visit him at his cabin."

“So he’s been harassing her for a while?”

“He has, and it’s gotten worse,” the nurse said. “I didn’t even feel comfortable around him before this happened. Now, I think I’m afraid.”

“I understand,” Leblanc said.

“Please don’t tell him that I told you where he lives, or anything about him. It will be much better if the clinic stays out of this, as he can be nasty, and none of us want to end up on his bad side, right now. We’re all scared.”

"I won’t mention your name at all,” Leblanc said.

He felt determined as he walked out of the clinic.

His next stop was going to be to interview the obsessive, unstable, and blonde-loving Kyle Davis, who was undoubtedly their most promising lead so far.

CHAPTER SEVENTEEN

The watcher hunkered down in his cabin. His lair, as he thought of it sometimes. A place away from the world, his private space, where he could be alone with his thoughts and his memories.

He had spent a long time preparing his hideout. There were no neighbors close by, and no one knew it was there. It was his place of safety. He had a lean-to behind the cabin where he parked his vehicles, an old Range Rover and a newer snowmobile. Leafy branches shielded the entrance so that they were basically invisible.

The cabin overlooked the lake. He found the view especially comforting in winter. There was something about the freezing blankness that soothed the demons in his mind.

He was glad his retreat was private. The watcher was not a popular person. He knew that. People thought he was weird. He knew that too. He'd become weirder as the years went by and the weak control he had over his thoughts began to slip away.

But no one knew about his thoughts. He had never told anyone about them. It was his secret, which he had managed to keep safe from the world.

Inside the cabin, he had what he needed for a basic life. He looked around him at his meager possessions. There was a bed, only one. It had come with a foldaway crib when he'd bought it from the secondhand store. He didn't have any children, so had never used it. Who would have allowed him to have children? He had never wanted any. How could he bring a child into a world that had allowed him to suffer so badly?

He had a little wooden table, a sink, a gas fireplace. There was a small kitchen counter where he prepared his meals. And the most important thing he had was a solid, thick door. A door that allowed him to shut the world out, and to shut himself in.

There was a pile of dirty clothes in one corner. The bottom of the pile was soaked with lake water. The rest of the clothing still had faint dark stains. He would have to take care of that, he decided. Perhaps he would cut through the ice, and scrub them and soak them in the lake until all the dark traces were gone.

Or it might be better just to throw them away.

Not near here, though. Somewhere else, where they would float away on the water and not float back to haunt him again.

He would think about that later, he decided. It was too cold to worry about cleaning clothes now.

On the shelf above the clothes, was a stack of books. Some were his; others he had borrowed. A few of the titles were familiar to him, others were more obscure and he was not sure what they were about. He had never read any of these books, but he would get around to them. Someday.

There was a tattered calendar, gray and disheveled, on the wall.

He didn't have any signage outside the cabin, as he had no visitors. No one could get to him. He was secluded here.

He liked being away from the world. It hadn't always been that way, because he remembered the times when he'd panicked about his solitary confinement. When every lonely second had felt like a lifetime as he had cowered in the dark, isolated and terrified.

Now, he realized he'd become too used to it. He was imprisoned in his loneliness. Sometimes, he felt bitter envy when he saw people living their lives in such a carefree way. Talking, laughing, making plans. Socializing easily, casually, as if they didn't have demons inside them, gnawing at their thoughts constantly.

But he knew he could change his life and break the chains that held him to his past. He had a plan and he was faithfully following the plan.

Inside the cabin, the walls were blank. He preferred it that way. But when he looked at them it was as if he saw the same face there, over and over. It was the face that was keeping him prisoner.

Just a couple of weeks ago he'd finally had the courage to do what he'd been thinking of for so long. He'd gone out and found her and then he had killed her. He'd thought it was over then, that he would be at peace, that the shadows in his mind would go away and he could make a fresh start.

The problem was that she hadn't died. He'd seen her again, the next time he'd gone into town. It had been a terrible feeling, as if he'd briefly been free of a burden that had returned to drag him down into the darkness again.

That freedom had been so short, so beautiful. He wanted it again, and he knew what he had to do. Kill her again. And, if necessary, again.

He thought he'd done it. He was sure. But again today, when he'd gone into town for supplies this morning, he had seen her again. His tormentor.

Those haunting blue eyes. That bright blonde hair. She was not yet dead, and he needed to find her. Because she had to be dead, otherwise she could hurt him again.

Feeling helpless anger seethe inside him, the watcher recalled a whispered conversation he had had with her when he was younger.

"You have to be careful," she had told him. "You have to protect our secret. Don't tell anyone or you know what will happen."

He remembered how she'd smiled when she had said that. Like it was a special secret. Not one that caused him pain.

He'd looked at her, searching her face for clues or for some trace of kindness or mercy.

"It's a shame you're so bad," she had whispered.

She was still smiling, but it was a different sort of smile. It was a cold, distant smile. It was a mean smile.

He could not erase that expression from his mind. It would be there forever. He knew he would never forget it as long as he lived. She had let him see the darkness in her eyes and in her soul.

"When I am finished with you, there won't be any more secrets," she had promised him. "You'll never do anything wrong again, only what I tell you to do."

He had become so fearful. He'd been afraid of his punishments, but even more worried that his parents would find out. If they were angry with her, he would suffer, and he knew his next punishment would be worse.

He felt as if he'd lived in a dark, haunted world of fear. But she had kept her promise. She had made sure no one found out.

And then, the worst had happened and his parents had died, killed in a car wreck on the way home. Then it had just been the two of them. He'd been in her care.

He remembered looking at his hands when he'd heard the news. They had started to shake, as if some invisible force had taken over his limbs. The whole world had spun around him and he couldn't stop it.

"He's sad. The poor little guy's so sad," the police officer had said sympathetically, but he didn't know the truth, that he had not been sad, but rather, afraid of what would happen next.

And it had gotten worse. He couldn't think about what she'd done, although the nightmares tormented him still. And he knew that he would not be free until he had killed her.

She couldn't keep coming back. Surely it was impossible for her to do that.

He had to leave the cabin and go back into town and find her. He was going to kill her again. He was going to make her suffer and then he was going to make her dead.

CHAPTER EIGHTEEN

By the time Katie reached the narrow, icy track that led to Zack's cabin, she was shivering with cold. The wind felt like icy knives against her skin. This cabin was remote, and although the building itself was sheltered by the trees beyond, the approach was in the teeth of the gale.

She wondered if Zack liked it this way. A man with PTSD and mental health issues might find a blank expanse of snow to be reassuring. He would know nobody was sneaking up on him. That might be important to someone like him.

At this time she should have a partner with her. It would be safer. But time and circumstances didn't allow for it, so instead, she sent Leblanc a quick message telling him what she was doing and giving her coordinates.

Then, she picked her way down the icy track to the cabin.

The pathway was short, only about two hundred yards. The cabin was a squat shape against the darkening sky. Snow was threatening yet again. Katie wondered what she would find inside. Would Zack be home? Would he be violent?

Was she approaching the killer's hideout?

Steeling herself to expect an unpredictable response, Katie followed the track over a rough wooden bridge and under a sweeping pine branch, heavy with snow. She saw the front door and walked up to it. There were two windows on either side but she couldn't see any lights on.

Pausing for a moment, Katie collected her thoughts, wondering if she should draw her gun. She decided against it, but loosened her coat so she would be able to grab it fast if she needed to. After all, she was going to confront a man who was known to be dangerous.

She knocked. There was no answer.

Katie shivered, glancing around this remote and empty wilderness.

She knocked again, louder this time. Still no answer.

"Open up, Zack," she shouted. "FBI. I need to speak to you."

Silence.

Inside, she could hear the tick of an old-fashioned clock.

She wondered if Leblanc had wrapped up on his side, because she might need help locating her suspect. He didn't seem to be home.

There was always the chance he was home, though, and just not answering her knock. Katie tried once more.

"Zack! We need information!"

Then Katie jumped as, from inside the room, she heard a crash and a thud.

He was there! Or somebody was!

"Open up!" she yelled again.

She didn't know what was awaiting her inside, but she couldn't delay a second longer. The more time that went by, the more the opportunities for Zack to get away, or else to arm himself in preparation.

Katie lifted her booted foot and slammed it firmly into the warped wooden door.

It flew open and she found herself standing in the open doorway of Zack's cabin.

Was he here, waiting for her? Or had he fled?

She stepped in, looking around, taking in every inch of the gloomy space. Her eyes were ready to pick up the slightest flicker of movement and her heart was thudding.

But the dimly lit cabin was empty.

The interior was even smaller than she'd imagined. The main room had a single bed and a camping cot. It smelled of wood smoke and raw fish.

There was a knife on the counter. That prickled her instincts.

She couldn't see any chess pieces. But there was something else that made her instincts sharpen as the faint, nauseating odor settled in her nostrils.

She took her phone out again and snapped the flashlight on to see what was there.

On the floor, the light picked up a splash of deep red. A trail of blood and guts, leading to the back of the cabin.

Katie drew in a deep, horrified breath and for a moment, visceral panic flared in her mind.

But even as she took in the bloody sight, her training kicked in. The protocols were ingrained in her mind. In this moment of high stress, she was able to damp down her fear and think rationally. She felt grateful for the high-pressure situations she'd been in, for the remorseless training that she'd undergone again and again, weak and sleep-deprived, but determined to succeed.

"Winter, don't panic. Think!"

Staring down, she thought. Her conclusion was that this didn't appear to be human blood or human guts. It seemed to be fish guts. There was an overturned bucket in the corner. So what had happened?

"Think, Winter!" her instructor's voice razored her mind again.

He'd been gutting a fish when she had knocked. That was all. He hadn't wanted to speak to the FBI so he had made a hasty escape, out of the tiny back door that she now noticed. She saw it was open a crack. The thick snow had allowed him to flee soundlessly.

Fleeing was a big red flag. Innocent people didn't run when law enforcement came knocking.

In one giant stride, she was out of the cabin's back door and fighting her way through the snow, following the deep footprints that led to the lake.

Zack had to be on the lake. He'd heard her coming and he'd run for it.

There he was. She saw him, a dark figure, moving over the ice.

The figure was moving rapidly, almost running. Undoubtedly, he was familiar with the lake and had gone out in these conditions many times before.

"Stop!" she yelled.

He hesitated. She was sure he'd heard. But he didn't stop.

Katie tried again, threatening him more seriously this time.

"Stop or I will shoot."

He turned to face her.

"You won't shoot! You're too afraid. Leave me alone. Or I'll shoot."

She didn't know how serious the threat was. She was about to reach for her gun when a sudden gust of wind picked up off the lake and churned the snow, making it hard to see. The snow whirled so thickly that Katie could feel it biting and stinging her skin.

Now, nobody could shoot, but this flurry was giving him the cover he needed.

He wasn't going to stop, and if this wind picked up, he could easily double back and lose her. She couldn't risk that and would have to chase him

"Zack! You'll be in trouble if you run!"

He didn't listen. She hadn't thought he would.

She stepped onto the ice and knew immediately that this was a bad idea. It didn't feel solid enough, and it was slippery and shifting. She could feel it cracking. All her instincts screamed at her to stop. This was the danger zone, the place where fault lines could spread in an instant and the lake could open into an icy, chilly grave. Pulled under by currents, a victim would either freeze or drown.

Carefully, step by step, she moved forward, feeling deeply uneasy about her decisions.

Katie couldn't let him get away, but she didn't want the both of them to drown. If this tall, heavy looking man continued to run, there was a very big chance that would happen.

"Stay where you are. You're not safe out there. The ice isn't strong enough."

She heard a slithering, cracking noise spreading across the lake. It was a sound she'd heard before and one she was instinctively afraid of.

"Stop moving. Please stop moving."

But Zack was running, running onto the frozen lake.

"Oh, oh no," Katie whispered.

The first sign of a crack had appeared beneath her. She could feel it, a vibration through the ice. It was like a living thing. She would be pulled in. She had to get off the ice, far back, as soon as she could.

Carefully, cautiously, she retreated, trying her best to keep him in her view.

And then all at once, she heard the crack, a terrible, thundering sound as the ice opened up, as if some giant were ripping the world in two.

He was going to go under, she thought, feeling the ice tremble and shift beneath her.

"Get back!" she yelled.

She saw him hesitate and knew he was weighing up his options and finding none. He was trapped between a certain, icy death, and herself.

She could hear the ice rumbling and splintering, and she saw a spray of ice crystals shoot up into the air and then smash down onto the surface of the lake.

She was still about fifty feet from the shore. It was too far. She was going to be sucked down into the water, too. Katie retreated more hurriedly.

At the last minute, Zack's nerve broke.

He turned and stumbled back toward her, flailing through a widening spider web of cracks.

Katie backed toward the shore, shuddering as much from cold as from fear. There wasn't much time. The ice was already weakened. At least he was returning and she could speak to him now.

But then, the worst happened. The ice opened up, spreading like a giant's jaws. The gap widened by the second, the frigid water seeping through the fissures.

The crack reached him, and swallowed him, and with a despairing yell, Zack plunged into the frigid water.

CHAPTER NINETEEN

Leblanc gritted his teeth as he clamped his hands on the wheel. It had been a long, cold and difficult drive to the remote cabin where Kyle Davis, the man who had harassed Gaby at the clinic, lived. Kyle stayed all the way at the end of the rutted track, and this last section was definitely the worst.

The car bounced and swayed. Leblanc realized that the snow had provided a thin layer over what was a massively eroded road. He couldn't see underneath. Could only ease the car forward.

He caught his breath as the SUV lurched sideways. Staring in horror out of the driver's window, he saw snow showering down a steep embankment. He was about to drive over the edge of a deep crevasse. The car started to shift, pulling to one side.

Leblanc's hands were sweating in his gloves. He slammed on the brakes, desperate not to lose control of the huge weight of the car. Easing the wheel to the side and inching forward, he prayed he could keep the SUV from rolling down the sharp incline.

Every teetering second seemed to take years off his life.

Imagine if he rolled the car here, in the middle of nowhere.

Leblanc let out a shaky breath of relief as the road smoothed out again and he saw the cabin ahead. This trip had been nerve-shredding, and he hadn't even gotten face to face with his suspect yet.

Activating the handbrake and hoping to hell the car didn't slide away down the crevasse where it clearly couldn't wait to go, Leblanc climbed out and stepped into knee-deep snow. He forged his way up to the cabin, keeping a good distance between himself and the front door. He had a bad feeling about this place. Looking at it, he felt as if he was walking into the lair of some troubled, fearful beast.

The cabin was a dilapidated building, its log walls fissured and peeling. It was covered with snow. A cracked, dusty pane of glass covered the only window he could see, effectively concealing what was inside.

Leblanc walked up to the door, his breath coming in white plumes.

"Kyle?" he shouted.

He waited, listening for a reply.

Kyle was not home. The place was empty. A padlock on the outside of the door was final proof that he was not inside. Was he out on the lake? The ice beyond the cabin looked bare. Leblanc couldn't see anyone in sight.

Another thought occurred to him. From what the nurse at the clinic had said, Leblanc hadn't thought to ask if this socially inept and abusive man worked. But perhaps he had a job. That was a possible explanation. Now that he had his first, and last name, he could track that information down.

Sighing, Leblanc turned and half-trudged, half-skidded back to his car.

It doesn't get like this in France, he thought with a flash of humor that surprised him, as he remembered Katie's curious look when he'd mentioned the country that had been home for most of his life.

He put the phone onto speaker, and dialed the number for the local Watertown PD, hoping they would be more competent when it came to tracking down a suspect's workplace than they had been in notifying the task force about a missing victim.

He edged the car back along the track. At least he knew where the crevasse was now.

"I'm looking to track down a suspect's workplace," he said when the officer answered, gritting his teeth as the car tipped sideways again. "Name's Kyle Davis." He gave the address he was driving away from.

"I'll call you back in a few minutes," the officer said. Unlike the bungling crime scene officers, she sounded sharper and more competent.

Leblanc passed the time constructively by gripping the wheel and trying to make progress along the track. He decided that although it didn't seem possible, the trip was actually worse on the way back.

He was glad of the distraction when the female officer called back.

"I have a workplace address for you," she said. "Kyle Davis works at the local sawmill. It's on the corner of Forest and Main."

"Thank you," Leblanc said. He shuddered as his car dropped down into a ditch and then bounced back.

"Is this all the information you're looking for?"

"For now, yes," Leblanc said.

He drove onto the snowy road and headed in the direction of Main Street.

He called Katie to check in with her. She didn't answer, and he felt a flare of worry. She'd sent coordinates and now she wasn't picking up. He left a message.

"I have a possible lead," he said. "Kyle Davis harassed Gaby at her work. He's employed at the sawmill on the other side of town. I'm heading over there right now. Call me if you need help urgently. Otherwise, I'll join you when I'm done."

*

The sawmill was housed in a huge, hulking building that looked like a giant factory. Leblanc parked his car and got out. As he walked to the entrance, his feet sank into the snow, and his breath steamed up the gloomy, gray sky.

Inside, the sawmill building was cavernous. The grinding of machinery was deafening. Leblanc heard the whine of circular saws and the screech of saw blades and the hissing of sanding machines. There was a multitude of beeping sounds as forklifts cruised back and forth over the enormous floor.

The smell of raw wood and fresh diesel hung in the air.

Leblanc hurried after a young man who was striding purposefully to a door on the side of the building. He caught up with him as he was about to head into the room, marked 'Manager's Office.'

"Excuse me," Leblanc shouted. He had to shout to be heard over the noise.

The man turned around, looking startled. He was in his late twenties, with a lean, pale face.

"What do you want? Sir, this is a working mill. You can't just walk inside. Did you not read the sign outside the door?"

Leblanc hadn't read the sign outside the door. He was too busy to read signs outside doors.

"I'm police. We're looking for Kyle Davis," he said. He reached into his pocket and pulled out his badge. "It's in connection with a murder investigation. I need to ask him some questions."

The man's eyes widened, and he hesitated.

"He's inside the stock room. He works as a stock clerk."

He pointed at a large door on the opposite side of the building.

Leblanc strode across the floor and pushed it open.

The stock room was enormous, but he spotted Kyle immediately, as he was the only occupant. He was hard at work, picking stacks of wooden pieces from a conveyor belt, and putting them on a pallet. He was a tall, strong man wearing faded jeans and a heavy black jacket. Easily six feet, Leblanc noted. A hat with ear flaps was pulled down low on his head.

"Mr. Davis," Leblanc called. "Detective Leblanc. I need to speak to you."

Whatever reaction he'd expected, it was not the one he got.

Kyle stared at him in horror.

Then, abandoning his stock count, he turned and ran out of the room's back door.

"Hey! Wait!" Leblanc shouted. “Come here! You’re disobeying an officer of the law!"

Kyle didn't stop. He was already out the door.

"Damn," Leblanc muttered, "Damn. Damn. Damn."

Sprinting past the humming conveyor belt and sliding over the sawdust on the floor, he set off in pursuit.

Kyle flailed and skidded as he ran out of the building’s front entrance and then doubled round the back. Leblanc followed him, dodging around lumber piles, past a huge loading dock, and between a double row of warehouses.

Kyle ducked into a narrow, rutted lane behind the sawmill. Leblanc sprinted determinedly after him. Kyle was fast, but Leblanc was gaining on him, his fitness and his determination giving him the edge.

Kyle was a big man but he was not a fit man. His gasps plumed into the air.

"Help!" Kyle shouted. "Someone, help me!"

"This is a police investigation!" Leblanc shouted back. "Stop running!"

But Kyle didn't stop. He kept running.

Except the lane ended a hundred yards ahead. It reached a dead-end, guarded by a high clapboard fence. Too high for Kyle to scramble over. He was trapped.

Kyle turned around and stared at Leblanc, his eyes wide and full of terror. His chest was heaving.

"What – what – do you want?" he said.

"I need to ask you some questions," Leblanc said. He was gasping, too, but trying not to let Kyle see how winded he was. He didn’t want him getting any ideas about running the other way.

"What's this about?"

"A series of recent murders."

Kyle's eyes flew wide.

"Oh!" he said. Leblanc couldn't read the expression on his face.

"You had a connection with a recent victim."

"I did?"

"Gaby Mackay. She worked in a clinic in town. You harassed her."

Now Kyle's eyes flew wider.

"Her? She's dead?"

Leblanc had expected him to sound surprised. What he didn't yet know was whether it was an act.

"Yes."

"Oh my God. Oh my God," Kyle wrapped his arms around himself, shaking his head violently.

"When was the last time you saw her?" Leblanc asked, not sure if he bought this shocked reaction. He didn't know how genuine his shock was, especially in view of the chase he'd just led Leblanc on.

"It was ages ago! Weeks ago. She wasn't there when I went to the clinic the last time."

"You harassed her at the clinic."

"No! I was just being friendly. And she didn't mind it. She was fine about it. I swear. We flirted together."

"Where were you last night?" Leblanc demanded, cutting to the chase.

"Last night?"

"Yes."

"I was – I was with my parents. I had nothing to do with this murder."

"The whole night?"

"Yes. They live in town. I took Mom grocery shopping and she got home at about six, and they said I must stay the night because my road's really bad after a storm."

Leblanc could attest to that, at least.

"Come with me," Leblanc ordered. He decided he was going to bring this suspect in. He was way too nervous for an innocent man. Leblanc was convinced that he was guilty, and trying to hide his involvement in these murders.

But then Kyle pulled out his phone. He unlocked it and practically threw it at Leblanc.

"Here," he pleaded. "Look here. This is the conversation between me and my mom. This is where she asked me to stay the night. And I even messaged the neighbor, to ask if I could park in her spot. She said yes. I thanked her again this morning when I left and I dug the driveway for her as well as my parents. It's all there. Please believe me when I say I'm innocent. It wasn't me."

Scrolling through the messages, Leblanc felt deflated. Pieced together, they did prove Kyle's whereabouts last night.

Leblanc had no doubt that Kyle was guilty of something. Whether it was possession of drugs, or illegal hunting, or some other breach of the law. That was why he'd run. But he couldn't have murdered Gaby and his time last night was accounted for.

This strong suspect could be ruled out, and with it, Leblanc's chances of solving the murder on his own and proving to Katie wasn't needed.

Thinking of Katie, he realized with a flash of alarm he needed to get to her immediately.

She still hadn't called back. What if something had gone wrong?

CHAPTER TWENTY

Frances Fick shivered, staring out at the snowy street. This cold was relentless, she thought. Having moved from Texas to Rochester for work in summer, she had no idea that the winter would be this harsh or this cold.

She loved her job. Hospitality was her calling. She'd jumped at the chance to manage this hotel, which was a step up from the inn she'd managed in Texas. This was a four-star hotel with a mix of leisure and business travelers, and it was usually well booked all year round.

Her hotel was the biggest in town. It was located on the lake, with a spectacular view of the town. It had a pool, a gym, a sauna, and a restaurant overlooking the lake. It had facilities for conferences, weddings, and banquets.

She loved her job, but – this cold! She wasn't sure she was ready for it every single winter. Perhaps it would be better to use this job as a stepping-stone and put her CV out again.

Looking at the TV set, she saw the weather channel was predicting more snow, harder cold, and temperatures dropping to minus five degrees Fahrenheit.

In mid-December! Everyone on the weather channel was shocked about this big freeze so early in the season, but all Frances could think was that she probably had another three months of this same unbearable cold.

She shivered again, and turned the TV off. She was not going to watch that, she decided. It was too depressing.

Frances walked over to a big, roll-top desk, took out a box of matches and lit the fire in the fireplace. The flames took hold, and she added a few logs, enjoying the cozy glow. The hotel's library, which was really a glorified meeting room, was on the street level and the warmest room in the hotel.

She pushed her blonde hair back from her face as she arranged the room, which would be used by a small conference group this afternoon. She was sure they would enjoy this atmospheric venue.

Checking her watch, Frances saw there was time for a coffee. She seldom took breaks at work, but today it seemed there was a spare twenty minutes for her to grab a hot drink in this secluded space.

She walked to the machine and poured herself a cup, and then sat down at the wooden table, enjoying the quiet, and the smell of the polished oak and rich coffee.

Except, for some reason, she started to feel as if something was wrong.

Turning, she stared at the big window, with its view of the snow-lined street outside.

Was that man watching her? He was standing in the street opposite the window and looking directly at the window.

He wore a hat, a heavy coat, and a scarf. Standing on the sidewalk, his feet seemed planted in the snow.

Was he staring at the library, or at her? It gave her a strange, creepy feeling to think he might be staring at her.

Suddenly, Frances realized how visible she must be from the street, in this brightly lit room.

She didn't like the feeling she had. Inexplicably, his gaze was chilling her as badly as the cold. She didn’t know why. Perhaps it was his stillness or the unwavering direction of his gaze.

Were there drug addicts in Rochester, she wondered. She hadn’t been exposed to that since she had arrived here. But this guy definitely seemed as if he was not normal.

Walking over to the window she pulled the blinds down. The guests would want to be private, she was sure. Even though the snow was starting to fall again, which would create its own curtain of privacy as activity slowly shut down on the street outside.

She didn't want the man to see her. She didn't like the feeling of being watched. She finished her coffee quickly. Then, heading back to reception, she checked the time.

"I'm going to head down the road and see if those table decorations for tonight are ready," she said to the receptionist.

"You sure you want to go now?" the other woman replied.

"Yeah, it will only take me a few minutes. I don't like driving when it's snowing hard. And I'll be back in plenty of time before the guests arrive."

"Okay," said the receptionist, without looking up.

Shivering again at the thought of venturing outside into this steely cold, Frances pulled on her hat and headed out, rushing to the old Chevy that she'd picked up for a bargain when she'd arrived in Toronto.

It held the road well but it wasn't a warm car. Cold filtered through the tiny gaps in the windows. It was basically like driving inside a fridge. She needed to upgrade it, and soon.

She climbed inside, slammed the door, and pulled on her gloves before turning the ignition key.

But, as she did so, she felt something, cold and hard against the back of her neck, in the gap between her jacket and hat. In a terrified breath, she realized it was the barrel of a gun, even as a man's voice sounded, deep and husky.

"Don't move, don't scream, or I will shoot."

But how could she not move, not scream? Fear surged in her veins, pumping adrenaline through her entire body. Logical thought abandoned her. She wanted to freeze, to become a statue in her seat, and for this impossible, terrifying thing to go away.

She was afraid to turn her head. She trembled with fear, her heart thundering in her ears, the ache in her breastbone spreading all through her body. Fear kept her frozen in place, too terrified to move a muscle, or cry out for help.

"Give me your phone," he said.

Now sobbing, she fumbled for it in her purse.

“I – I can’t find it.”

He wanted her phone and she couldn’t find it. It was the guy she’d seen earlier. She was sure of it; he was a drug addict and could turn violent at any moment.

“H – help!” she cried in a wavering voice.

"Quiet. Or I'll shoot!" the man threatened. “Give it to me and everything will be fine.”

Frances sobbed. She managed to get her fingers around the phone and pull it out of her purse.

The man suddenly grabbed her hand, and wrenched her wrist, and the phone, around so that he could reach it.

He had her phone. Now, would he go? She still felt the coldness of the gun at her nape.

"Now, I need you to drive."

"D-drive?" She didn't know if she could manage, she was shaking so hard. "Where?" she asked.

"Where I tell you," he replied. "I need a ride.”

“Take my car,” she suggested. She didn’t want to go with him. Warnings from long ago came to her. In a situation like this, you should always try to get away. Going with a carjacker was a bad idea.

If she was brave enough, she could grab the door handle and leap out. She might make it out of the car before he shot at her, if she could be fast enough and surprise him. Especially if she did it with another car approaching. Then the driver would see her and know something was wrong.

Frances tensed.

But she couldn’t. Not with the gun pressing up against her neck. It seemed like too much of a risk. And the oncoming car was going too fast. If she jumped out now it would skid on the icy road. Most probably she’d be hurt.

The car swished by and with it, the opportunity. Cold fear clenched inside her again.

“I won’t hurt you. Go north, down the road,” the man urged her.

She had no options left.

With tears stinging her eyes, Frances started up the car and set off, following an erratic route down the main street, hoping that if she complied, her life might be spared.

CHAPTER TWENTY ONE

Crouched in the back seat, the watcher kept the gun pressed to the blonde woman's head, its barrel nestling in between her thick, golden locks. He felt calm and focused. It was good to be speaking to someone again, even if it was to his tormentor. It was the first time he'd risked a scenario where he'd let her drive. He'd missed having a conversation. Even his voice sounded rough, as if he hadn't used it enough. Not the way he wanted it to sound, but he had no choice.

"Turn right at the stop sign," he told her.

He could hear her sobbing. Her driving felt shaky and uneven. Perhaps, at last, she felt sorry for what she'd done to him. That would be good, he thought, feeling a moment's confusion as his thoughts scattered.

Then, the quick movement of her head refocused them again.

"Don't turn around. You look straight ahead, and concentrate on your driving," he warned.

It was so quiet in the car now. He loved the feel of the gun against her nape. He loved the way she trembled. He could feel her shaking, even through the leather of the seat.

But he couldn't believe he was having to kill her again. Why, oh why, did she keep coming back? It felt like she was haunting him.

The woman was sobbing again now, whispering over and over: "Please, don't hurt me, please don't hurt me." He understood. He had sobbed that way, too. He had also begged. He was glad that now, she knew how it felt.

"Turn right here. Be careful. This is a rough track," he warned.

She was calmer now, he could feel it. He could tell that she was staring ahead, concentrating and doing as he ordered.

"I don't want to hurt you," he muttered.

It had all been a game to her, he knew that. How could anyone be so cruel? Why was she so scared now, when she had tormented him so badly?

"You can stop now," he said.

She pulled the car to a halt. He took the gun from her neck and climbed out. He heard her sobbing quietly as he approached her side of the car. He opened the door.

"Step out," he commanded.

He was pleased that she was doing as he said. She'd learned. It must mean she was sorry for what she'd done before.

"Can I go?" she asked. "Please, take the car. Let me go."

He looked at the snow-covered tracks, at the snaking lane that was barely visible under the snow.

"We're walking from here," he said. "Just walk. We're going to the lake. Don't run!"

But even as he said that, with a cry of fear, she turned and ran, slipping and sliding down the icy track.

"I'm not going to the lake!" she cried. "I know who you are. I read about you online! You're the killer who's been murdering women!"

The words struck him like daggers. How could she say that? After all he'd been through at her hands?

And now she was running. Her words had stopped him. Paralyzed him. Now he had to catch up, and fast.

The watcher scrambled down the slope after her. He could hear the crackle and crunch of her running through the snow.

He ran after her, cursing her. Cursing himself.

She was faster than he'd expected her to be. But he was determined and strong, and used to running in the snow.

"Come back! You're not allowed to run!"

She'd reached the lake. It didn't stop her. She fled out, across the ice.

Grasping his gun, the watcher stared after her, and a thought occurred to him, so logical and persuasive that it stopped him in his tracks.

Maybe he'd been doing it wrong all this time, he decided. Maybe that was why she kept coming back. Perhaps this time, if he shot her, she would stay dead.

Aiming the gun carefully, summoning all his will, he pulled the trigger.

The blast sounded shockingly loud in the quiet. He knew immediately it was a mistake and his fear surged. He couldn't make mistakes.

She had fallen, but not in the right place. Blood was already staining the ice, and the snow was not heavy enough to hide it. He'd been an idiot. He hadn't waited till dark, till the heavy snowfall he needed. That had been her fault. She'd tricked him into it.

Picking her up, he half-lifted and half-dragged her further out onto the ice. He had what he needed. His knife, for the ritual. The chess piece, the wood pressing into his breast pocket. This time he'd chosen the rook. Perhaps this piece, with its strong, tower-like shape and tiny battlements, would work and stop her from coming back.

Quickly, he did what he needed, feeling frantic that he might be caught, that someone had heard the shot. It wasn't as satisfying as the last time he had done it. It wasn't as neat. He had wanted the scene to look perfect.

The ice wasn't thin enough for her to sink into the lake. He couldn't make the scene perfect, like he wanted it to be.

Clutching his knife, he turned and away.

And then, with a horrified intake of breath, he saw the figure who had been staring at him by the shore.

"No!" he shouted, his agonized voice echoing across the frozen lake. The watcher felt his heart thumping. There had been a witness. Another person had seen. He only knew one thing: he had to get to this man before he got away.

He ran back over the uneven ice, his legs heavy with fear, his breath coming in harsh gasps. He tripped, almost fell, and righted himself.

But the man ahead of him was faster. He disappeared over the crest of a hill and a moment later, he heard the scream of a snowmobile engine.

He stood, his head bowed, feeling the horror of this fill him.

A witness.

He'd been recognized and seen.

Fear thrilled through him as he imagined the police knocking on his door. They wouldn't understand his reasons and he had to escape them. He needed to hole up and hide now but he'd killed her too close to home this time. That was another, bad mistake.

Then he had an idea. A crazy plan, born of sheer desperation.

If he killed one final time, made the scene perfect, placed it in a nearby area, perhaps he could misdirect them and they would never find him at all.

CHAPTER TWENTY TWO

As Katie watched in horror, Zack plunged down into the icy lake. This was it, she thought. If he was guilty, they would never know. And if he was innocent, she'd caused his death.

But then, to her astonishment, she saw he was only partway submerged. He must have broken through the ice on one of the long sandbanks that stretched out into the lake in this area.

Up to his waist in freezing water, he was shouting and struggling, plunging forward.

Katie looked around, frantically searching for something she could use to help him out.

There, near the icy border of the lake, was a broken tree branch, leafless and jagged.

Grabbing it, she headed cautiously toward him.

"Hold on!" she yelled. "I'm coming!"

Zack was struggling to get out of the water. His hands were scrabbling on the ice, trying to pull himself out.

“Can you get hold of this?”

Creeping forward as close as she dared, picking her way through the solid ice and avoiding the crack, she held out the branch. His hands must be totally numb by now, she feared. But he managed to grab it.

She held onto it with all her might as he flailed and scrambled out of the icy water. He was shuddering with cold.

"Don't tell me to lie down on the floor," he gasped, looking at her with a mix of suspicion and fear. "I can't lie down. I'm too cold!"

“We need to go back to your cabin,” Katie said. “I have to ask you some questions, but let’s get you warm first, and fast.”

"I want to get warm," Zack was gasping with the cold.

“Keep moving. You'll be all right, I promise. Let's get out of the wind,” she reassured him, thinking how strange it was that the tables had turned. He was too chilled to run. That was good. So now, all she had to do was guide him back to his cabin. In a few more steps, she would learn the truth.

At the cabin, she helped him inside. He looked like a drowned rat. His face was blue. His wet clothes had already frozen onto him, and his teeth were chattering.

She pulled off his coat and shirt, took off his boots and socks. His clothes were filthy. Even half-frozen, they stank. But at least he was warm now. She passed him a threadbare blanket as he turned to the fireplace and, with shuddering hands, clumsily lit a small fire.

Its smoky aroma filled the room.

"What do you want?" he said, looking confused and aggressive all over again as his strength returned.

"I want to ask you some questions. I'm FBI. There was a murder near here. A few murders."

"No! It wasn't me!" Zack shouted. "You're going to frame me. I can tell! This is what I've always known would happen!"

He wasn't thinking clearly. He was paranoid and delusional, Katie saw. But was he the killer? His shoes were the right size. He was tall enough. She didn't know how far his alternative reality stretched.

She saw the wildness in his eyes, the agitation.

"I'm not trying to frame you," Katie said firmly. "I want to clear you, Zack. Where were you last night?"

"I was here, of course. I don't go out. At night, I shut down my phone, because Big Government owns the airwaves. I stay home. I stay inside. I wrote in my journal. I can show you!"

Sounding more confident now, he bunched up his blanket and pulled out a well-thumbed notebook.

"I can show you!" he repeated. "This is my journal!"

"All right," Katie said. "Show me."

The book was filled with neat, small writing, but as neat as the script was, the ideas were chaotic. His thoughts were rambling and incoherent, interspersed with sections where he related his daily actions.

"Here's yesterday." He pointed, with a dirty finger. "I wrote that last night."

Katie looked down. The page was headed with yesterday's date. It was filled with a rambling account of his fishing activities, and how he'd had a quiet day, and how he thought he'd stayed safe from the agents and - ironically, she saw - avoided the FBI. In the journal he'd listed his dinner: a fish, caught in the evening and cooked over an open fire.

"That's all?" Katie said. She was disappointed. She'd been hoping for something else, something more concrete that could either clear him or incriminate him. She paged back, looking for any evidence of murderous intent in these detailed pages, but all he wrote about was hunting, fishing, his home improvements, hints on making fur clothing, and avoiding Big Government.

"After I finished writing, I went to bed. That's all."

Even going to bed was written down, she saw. He'd noted his hours of sleep and the level of snowfall. He'd done the same every night. This notebook was a record of his life.

"I'm not a killer. I just want to live in peace, away from everyone. I've never hurt anyone."

"I heard you chased people, and threatened them. That's what brought me here."

Zack paused. "Yeah, sure. I chased trespassers off my land."

"Trespassing on your land?"

"My land, my space. This is my cabin. I live here. I have a right to privacy! It's my right! I don't leave this area. I haven't left for years. I don't even own a car. I don't even own a snowmobile. Look outside. I don't have one. I stay here and mind my business, but I don't like people coming here."

"Why did you run when you saw me?"

"I knew you were government from the time you hammered on my door. I don't want to talk to you! I don't trust you. I don't trust any of you!" He was breathing heavily. "I told you. I'm self-contained, I don't need anything from anyone. No one should be able to get to me."

"Do you play chess? Own a chess set? Whittle chess pieces?" she asked him suddenly.

Staring at her, she saw only total confusion on his face.

"Chess?" he asked incredulously. "No, why?"

She should have gotten a different reaction from that question and she hadn't.

That was the final evidence she needed. He hadn't shown any knowledge of the chess pieces, and he didn't own a car or any other motorized vehicle. Whoever had murdered these victims had covered a wide area and would have needed to drive over the snow numerous times over the past week. She was going to make the decision that this was not their guy.

As Katie walked despondently out of the cramped shack, she saw Leblanc approach.

"You sent coordinates," he asked. "Everything okay?"

Katie nodded. "Everything is fine. I caught the suspect, but he didn't check out. He's a survivalist," Katie said. "Very insular. He doesn't like people."

"But he's not the killer?"

"He doesn't own a vehicle of any kind. The killer would have needed transport. And he knew nothing about the signatures." She looked at him questioningly. "What about you? Any progress on the suspect you mentioned?"

Leblanc shook his head, disappointed.

"His alibi checked out. I called the other patients who were hunters or fishermen and who were at the clinic in the past two weeks, but none of them could have done it. Either they have alibis, or injuries that put them out of the running."

"Okay, then," she agreed. "Let's get out of here."

As they headed toward the car, she saw Zack staring out of his cabin window at her. If looks could kill, she thought to herself, she'd be dead. He didn't appreciate the involuntary bath he'd taken in the lake, thanks to Big Government.

"So we're back to square one." Leblanc stated baldly.

Katie felt disappointment fill her, but also resolvc. There were other fishermen out there. It felt like an endless task, but if combing the entire shoreline was what it took, that was what she would do.

"I didn't think your theory would check out," Leblanc said, and to her annoyance she detected a smug note in his voice. How peaceful it had been, going on her own for a while, she thought with an inward eye-roll.

"I didn't think you'd be on the right track either," she retorted, ready for an argument.

"Maybe it's not a fisherman at all," Leblanc said, more conciliatory now. "Maybe it's someone else altogether."

Katie shook her head. "I don't think so," she said. "It has to be someone who is local, and mobile, and familiar with the area."

At that moment, her phone rang. It was Clark on the line and he sounded panicked.

"You won't believe this. There's just been another kill. A woman's body has been dumped at the lake, south of Rochester. Locals were alerted when they heard a gunshot."

Katie felt stunned. This was not what she'd expected. This killer was accelerating his agenda.

She'd been expecting he would prepare to kill again, but not yet. Why would he start killing at such a close interval? It hadn't even been snowing hard.

What could have happened? What could have made him start killing now?

And using a gun? He'd never done that before. Was it even the same killer or was this a copycat crime, or a domestic violence incident?

"Let's go see," Leblanc said, sounding as discouraged as she now felt.

They got in their car, and Leblanc drove up the road, through the forest and past the cabin on the edge of the lake. The snow had started again. The world outside the car was white and still.

Frustration built inside her as the car bumped over the ruts in the road.

Rochester was close by, but with the unforgiving terrain it would take them another half-hour to get there. If this proved to be another serial crime, it meant the killer was ahead of them, and gaining.

CHAPTER TWENTY THREE

It felt like a white-out eternity before Katie and Leblanc reached the road leading to the new crime scene. She felt filled with tension at what she might find. There were so many variables and time was not on their side.

"This might not be the same killer if he used a gun," Leblanc warned, as they headed down the track. Already she could see the crime scene tape ahead, and the flashing red and blue lights, bright in the white.

"It could be someone different. Either a coincidence, or someone is using the string of murders as a cover for another crime. In a way, I hope it's that, because the other possibility is that our killer's interval is shortening drastically."

"It had better not be shortening this fast," Leblanc said worriedly.

Stepping off the track, he skidded and almost fell.

"Wait," he called to her. "Watch the ground, it's steep here."

She nodded, and scrambled down the hill toward the knot of figures waiting there.

Katie paused, staring at the scene before her.

The body hadn't yet been removed, and the scene was frozen, preserved in the white snow. The first thing she saw, out on the lake, was the trail of blood, crimson and stark. It was a terrible sight.

Katie moved forward, her shoes crunching on snow. The police murmured greetings to her and Clark bustled over from where he'd been making calls near his car.

"Forensics is still on their way. They were held up due to the weather. Involved in a car wreck," Clark told her, sounding frazzled. "He must have carjacked the victim. We found an abandoned vehicle further down by the road. The tracks lead away from it. Johnson and Anderson are already on the way back with the details. They're going to trace the plate now, and they will then follow that lead and see if there were any witnesses."

Katie stared down at the red snow, the bright blonde hair. She shivered.

Was it the same killer?

Moving forward, she peered down and looked between the woman's blue lips, which were slightly parted. Her heart sped up as she saw the wooden piece there. She couldn't see which one it was, only its rounded and slightly uneven base. But it was his signature. His kill.

"This is the serial murderer's work. But it's a departure from what he's done before," she said, wondering why and wishing she could outthink him.

"Why do you say that?" Leblanc asked.

"For a start, he used a gun. He's never done that before. He killed in broad daylight, when there were other people around and he didn't wait for a heavy snowfall. Is he panicking? Getting impatient? Did he make a mistake? There has to be a reason why he did things differently this time."

Leblanc nodded thoughtfully. "Could he be taunting us? Daring us to catch him?"

"I don't think he's in control," Katie said. "I think he's out of control. Killing in daylight is massively risky. I think he's starting to panic."

"Why do you say that?" Leblanc asked. He sounded curious, rather than arrogant this time, she noted.

As Katie got ready to tell him more about the killer's possible state of mind, Clark's shout interrupted them.

"Look here," he yelled. "There are tracks here. And they're still fresh!"

Katie's heart accelerated. Could it be that the killer's haste would prove to be his downfall? At last, they seemed to have gotten a break. They could find out where he went.

She and Leblanc hurried over, each jostling to be ahead of the other.

"I see smaller footprints. Those must be hers. Perhaps she ran from him and he chased her. And others, here. I recognize the tread," she said excitedly. "These are the same boots he used at the last scene."

She couldn't believe it. After all this time, they had a break.

"There's blood here, too," she saw. "I think he shot in the back and she fell."

"And then he carried her out to the lake," Leblanc suggested. "And then, he fled. Here are the prints going the other way."

"It looks like he was in a rush. He was running."

Katie peered down at the tracks.

"Why would he run away from the scene?" Leblanc said.

“That’s a very good question.” The cogs were turning in Katie’s mind as she visualized what might have played out.

“He was seen,” she concluded, as they scrambled over the icy ridge, following the tracks. “Someone heard the shot and then noticed him carrying something out to the lake. He was in a hurry, he messed up, he panicked. He’s not thinking clearly. When he saw someone had seen, he gave chase, but –”

As she crested the ridge, the evidence was there.

“Snowmobile tracks. This guy got away in a hurry and I don’t blame him. He was being chased by a killer with a gun.”

“His tracks disappear on this pathway,” Leblanc said, sounding disappointed. “That’s hard ice there. No sign of prints. And it splits into three directions.”

Katie nodded. “But it means we have a witness. If we find the witness, they might know which direction the killer headed. I don’t think the witness would have tried to do anything clever. He was panicking and looking to hide. He would have taken the quickest route out of here.”

"Someone might have seen the snowmobile. People fish here," Clark observed.

"Why don't we ask the people who are at the scene now?" Leblanc suggested.

Katie glanced back. In her preoccupation with the body, she hadn't realized that a few scattered onlookers were gathering, standing on the snow, attracted to the scene by the flashing lights and crime scene tape.

She walked over to the nearest person, a middle-aged man wrapped up in an enormous coat, with a hat pulled down so low it almost obscured his bushy eyebrows.

“Did you see anyone leave in a hurry, on a snowmobile, about half an hour ago?” she asked.

The man looked back at her. He shook his head. “I was fishing on the other side of the ridge, and didn’t see anything this side.”

Katie turned and saw another man standing on the edge of the crowd.

"Did you see anyone ride away from here on a snowmobile?" she asked him.

He nodded hesitantly. Katie felt determination flood her.

"What did you see?" she pressed.

The man looked doubtful.

"I did see someone, riding away from the lake. I think he lives in the small cottage, over there, on the other side of the road going past the shore. But I know him well. He's not a killer. He's a good guy. Please, don't make trouble for him."

Glancing at Leblanc, Katie turned and began striding purposefully toward the road.

"It couldn't have been him!" the man called plaintively behind them.

Katie raced across the snow. Her goal was the small white house on the other side of the road, where the man was pointing.

With Leblanc close behind her, she jumped down the slippery bank, and hurried across the snowy road. Her feet sank into drifts of snow as she dashed to the house.

The snowmobile tracks led around the cottage, to the back, and it looked as if the man had tried to do a hasty cover-up at the place where they'd left the road.

He'd been scared and running, she thought.

Leblanc hammered on the peeling, dented wooden door.

"Who's there?" a fearful man's voice replied.

"Police! We need to ask you questions, sir."

"Police? Do you have ID?" This man was seriously shaken. Katie realized he had run for his life. If he'd been slower, there could have been two bodies waiting for them on the ice.

"We have ID," she called, hoping that a woman's voice might make a difference. "I'm Special Agent Katie Winter. I'm with Detective Leblanc. What's your name?"

There was a pause.

The door was opened a few inches. The man didn't open it more, but stuck his face out instead. He looked to be in his sixties, with a deeply lined and weathered face.

"My name's Mike Anders. What is it? What do you want?"

"We're investigating the recent murder at the lake. Witnesses saw you leaving the scene, and we believe you might have seen the killer."

The door opened wider.

"I think I saw someone shoot a woman," the man muttered. "I've never seen such a thing here. I was shocked, and then, as soon as he saw me, he started running. He had a gun and I didn't want to be next. I holed up in here. I was going to call you, but my phone's out of battery and the power's still out after the storm," he explained.

"What did the man look like?" Katie asked, feeling a thrill of excitement that finally, they had a lead.

"Tall. A big guy. It was difficult to see more. He was all wrapped up."

"Did you see which direction he went afterward? Perhaps you looked outside to make sure he wasn't coming after you? We can't trace his tracks back further than the pathway so we'd appreciate any help."

The man paused, then nodded.

"Yes. I did look out. I was very worried he'd come for me. I can show you, if you're sure he's gone now."

"He's fled. But we are going to catch him," Katie promised.

They walked back across the road. Anders scrambled up over the hill and then he pointed to the south.

"He stood here for a while. He was looking around to see if he could see me. I was hiding inside, hoping that he wouldn't see the tracks from my snowmobile. There was something really creepy about him. Something that made me feel trapped, instead of safe. Then he turned and he walked away in this direction."

He pointed south and Katie felt a flash of triumph. They were going to close in on him now. At some stage, if they followed the path south, they might pick up his prints again, and now they knew in which direction he was hiding out.

This was their best chance so far. They were on his trail, but with a storm threatening, she knew they didn't have much time.

CHAPTER TWENTY FOUR

Leblanc forged through the untrodden snow to the south, staring at the path, hoping to pick up the sole treads that were now familiar to him with their deep, slanted pattern.

Katie was soldiering behind him in his tracks.

He looked around. The snow had piled up here. Thanks to the blowing wind, there were drifts up to two feet deep. The snow felt cold against his legs. He hadn't thought it possible to add any more layers of clothing but now he was realizing how fast the cold ate through the flimsy fabric, nibbling his skin with icy jaws.

He pulled his coat tight around him.

Ahead, the woods loomed. And looking down, he saw the trodden path had disappeared. A massive bank of snow had collapsed ahead, obliterating it.

"I can't see it," he said worriedly.

"He must have gone into the woods," Katie said. "That's where he is. There are no other tracks. Perhaps it was his footsteps that dislodged the snow, if he was running in a panic."

"We could go back. Get backup and come here with a few more people. Do a proper search," Leblanc suggested, but he already knew that idea wasn't going to fly. Sure enough, Katie shook her head.

"We have such a small window of time to catch him," she pointed out.

Going back would be more sensible, but she was right about the time, and he didn't want to give up, either.

Was the killer hiding in the woods? Leblanc knew he would have to consider that they might be walking into an ambush. This man had already tried to chase a witness. He and Katie would have to be careful, especially since he had a gun.

Leblanc was almost at the woods when the wind hit him, slamming him sideways as if he'd been shoved. The warmth bled out of him as the cold ripped through layers that had seemed so bulky and warm when he'd put them on. His eyes stung with the cold, and the snow swirled around him. Staggering sideways, he saw Katie recoil as it hit her.

"Winter by the lake. Fun times," she said ruefully. "Hopefully this is a wind tunnel and we'll be protected from it in the woods."

They walked deeper into the trees, pushing aside branches and shoving snow aside. Leblanc thought he'd picked up the trail again, but it was more difficult to follow here. He scoured the snow to see where the faint tracks went. But, in the trees, they became increasingly impossible to see.

He'd fled to the woods and he'd managed to vanish.

"We need to cast around. There must be prints somewhere," Katie said, frustrated.

"Do you think he went this way?" Leblanc asked, pointing to a scuffed patch of snow. Did that look like a footprint? He couldn't tell.

"It's possible," Katie said, bending forward to examine the snow. As she did so, Leblanc felt aware all over again of how vulnerable they were to someone watching.

All his senses were prickling, knowing this man had a gun. Snow spattered him, falling coldly onto his face. Had a tree moved? Why the sudden shower, Leblanc wondered, tensing.

Suddenly, he heard a deafening creak. It didn't sound like the wind. He looked up, fear coiling inside him.

Behind them, not ten feet away, a tree was falling.

"Look out!" he shouted, racing forward and grabbing his partner's arm. He tugged her out of the way. They dived to safety as the tree toppled over with an impact that shook the ground, sending up a massive shower of snow.

They both fell, tumbling across the snow, before they came to a stop.

He was panting, winded by the impact.

"Katie!" he gasped. Where was she?

"Here," she said, sitting up and shaking a layer of snow away.

"Are you okay?"

"I'm okay."

Leblanc looked down. If there had been any tracks, the spray of snow from the branches would have completely obscured them. Now, how could they backtrack and check with a giant tree blocking the way?

Feeling numb with cold and chilled with discouragement, he examined his options. There didn't seem to be many. They were stranded in the woods and had lost the trail.

But then Katie grabbed his arm. "Look."

She pointed at the ground, where there were footprints leading off to the right beyond the shower of snow.

"He didn't go further ahead. I think he's doubled back," Katie said. She paced in that direction, looking intent. "See? There are new tracks, leading past the trees to the right."

"Are you sure?" he asked, frowning at the uneven dents.

Katie took her glove off, and with her hand she felt for the prints in the snow.

"What are you doing?" he asked. She'd get frostbite in seconds.

"I'm feeling for them. We used to do this as a game, when we were kids."

Moving forward, she felt again.

"Here we go."

The trail veered right and then sharply left. Finally, to Leblanc's extreme relief, she put her glove back on.

Now the prints were clear. This was a more sheltered part of the forest. The prints were far apart as if the man was walking fast, or even running. In the deep snow, that meant he was fit and used to the terrain.

Another pile of snow fell from an overhanging branch, making them both jump.

Leblanc pulled his revolver out of its holster, kept the safety on, and then continued forward. He kept his ears open for any sound of movement, and scanned the trees, blinking as he walked because his eyes were watering from the cold and the cutting wind.

Katie hesitated. She turned, staring into the darkening woods.

"What is it?" Leblanc asked.

"I thought I saw a figure there. In the trees. But it was so dark and so fleeting, I'm not sure. I could have imagined it."

Goosebumps prickled his back as he stared in the direction she had pointed out.

"The trees are thick," she went on. "There's a lot of brush around here. It's hard to see past the deadfall. If someone was out there, it would be easy to hide, and if they came up behind us, we wouldn't see them."

"We just have to be careful," he said quietly.

The snow was still blowing all around, but the wind itself had stopped. The hairs at the back of his neck prickled. He knew this silence couldn't last. It was a lull before the storm.

He looked back. Katie was a few yards behind him. She looked suddenly vulnerable against the threatening darkness.

But ahead, he saw a clearing. They had reached the edge of a large meadow that stretched far into the distance. The snow was lighter here. They had reached the leeward side of the storm and the tracks were now visible and even again.

The bad news was that they led up to a communal pathway that was filled with footprints. On the well-trodden ground, his prints were now obscured. They would have to follow the trail and see if they could find them again.

The sky was darkening, and out of the protection of the woods, the wind was blowing harder again. Katie looked around. The snow was falling faster, the flakes swirling around them. Soon, they wouldn't be able to see anything.

The sensible option would be to go back and radio for help. Glancing at Katie, Leblanc saw she was not ready to do anything so logical, and nor was he.

He could see she was determined. Stubborn was another word he might have used to describe both of them.

"How do we do this in the fastest way?" he asked.

"Divide and conquer?" she asked, quirking her head humorously. "We'll need to split up. I go left, you go right?"

Leblanc hesitated. "We know this guy has a gun. We should stick together."

"It's risks versus benefits," Katie argued. "And right now, the risk of him getting away is higher. We can't lose any more time. Especially since his killing interval is shortening."

Looking grim, Leblanc took in the hard truth of her words. "I guess you're right," he said.

"Sounds good," she said, nodding in a pleased way that her partner was on the same page.

She strode away, scanning the ground purposefully. Leblanc stared after her. He felt worried, and then surprised at himself for being so concerned about his headstrong partner.

Hadn't he wished, just a few hours ago, that he could pursue this case on his own? Now he was seriously invested in his partner's safety and wondering if it would have been a better idea for them to keep together.

He knew what the hunters and survivalists in this area were like. Even he, as a man, wasn't always comfortable approaching them, and he had no doubt their attitude to a female law enforcement officer would be far worse.

And those were the men who were innocent of this crime. This killer was far more dangerous and ruthless, and Leblanc feared he would stop at nothing to protect himself.

"I need to catch him. Guy's done enough damage," he muttered, hoping the strong words would go some way to suppressing the thrill of fear he felt as he set off along the icy, uneven track.

CHAPTER TWENTY FIVE

Heading along the trail, Katie kept her gaze focused on the path in front of her, occasionally raising her head to stare around and check out the frozen landscape for any sign of threat.

The only sounds were the crunch of ice and snow underfoot, the low moan of wind, and the occasional yelp from a distant dog.

The killer was wise to the area and to the lake and woods. She had to stay alert because otherwise she wouldn't see him until it was too late.

He might have run away. He might even have doubled back. Or he might have stayed in the trees, waiting to ambush her.

Staring down at the rutted ice, she hoped she might somehow pick out his tracks in the hard, slippery, compacted ground.

She kept her eyes on the ground, looking for any sign of a footprint or indentation.

Her thoughts strayed to Leblanc, following the path to the east even as she was heading west. She hoped he was also staying alert, and that he would stay safe. She didn't want him to be hurt.

The trees stopped swaying, and the swarm of snowflakes stopped swirling. Katie lifted her head and looked around.

The air was perfectly still. The silence echoed all around, sending shivers down her spine.

Katie felt a prickling sensation at the back of her neck, and she stopped, turning around and looking behind her, alert for any noise.

She had the feeling she was being watched even though there was no sound but the low moaning of the wind.

A chill froze her skin and the hairs prickled at the back of her neck. She searched the woods, straining her ears and looking for any sign of movement. Had one of the trees moved? The branches were still, but she was sure she'd seen a shadow.

But even though she strained her eyes, nothing more was clear.

Shrugging off the feeling of threat, she tried to focus on the path in front of her.

The wind increased, whipping the snow into her face, cutting into her like icy needles, and stinging her hands as she tried to brush it away.

There. A couple of hundred yards ahead of her, she saw a building. Squat and wooden, it looked grim in its starkness but its log walls looked solid. She saw a faint plume of smoke rising from the chimney.

She set off, weaving through the trees, watching the building in front of her as she approached.

What would she find in this small cabin? Had he taken shelter in there?

Katie stopped, surprised, as she saw a man appear in the doorway. He was clad in a heavy winter coat, boots, and a hat. He was bearded, and his shoulders were broad. He was holding a hunting rifle. He saw her and looked startled.

"Hey there," she said, her stomach churning. She couldn't afford to show fear. Not at this stage.

The hunter watched her approach. She felt his eyes on her. The wind was howling around her, but even so, she felt a trickle of cold sweat run down her spine.

This was the first building she had seen. If he had been heading away from the lake, she would have expected him to hide out here.

The hunter turned back and said something she couldn't hear, to someone else inside. Quickly, Katie walked closer.

"FBI Agent Katie Winter," she introduced herself politely. "We're following the trail of a murder suspect."

He nodded, but didn't answer. Another man appeared from the lodge doorway, standing and facing her, and then another walked out.

The three men stood in front of the log cabin. All of them were dressed for the weather, with heavy winter coats and hats. They looked at her with cold, suspicious faces. Katie felt immediately that they were closing ranks. All her suspicions flared.

She knew about the survivalists in this area. They were tough men, hard men, who lived by their own laws. From when she was very small, her father had given her and Josie dire warnings about avoiding them. Some of the warnings had given Katie nightmares.

"Yes?" one of them said.

Katie hesitated. "I need your help. I'm tracking a killer. We followed his footprints and he might have passed by here."

"No," the man said. "We've seen nobody."

"He's armed and dangerous," she added, making sure they knew what they were dealing with. "He's suspected of three murders, and possibly more."

The men stared at her, but still didn't say anything.

Katie walked closer, wondering if there was anyone else inside.

Glancing beyond them, she saw the sparse interior of the hunting lodge. A fire smoldered in the grate. A lantern hung on one wall, and a rifle was propped up against another, while a single bed was shoved into the far corner. A pile of logs was stacked next to a pile of kindling.

Nobody was hiding inside.

But all these men were tall. All were strong, and any could be the killer.

"Have you seen him?" she asked again, trying to break through their resistance.

Her words had the opposite effect.

"Get lost, lady. He didn't come this way. If he did, who cares? We don't like law enforcement," the tallest man said.

"You don't like murderers? People who grab women in town and then kill them in cold blood?" She hoped her words would have an effect.

The man looked down. Then he shrugged. "We didn't see anyone come this way."

"Who are you?" she asked. "What are your names?"

"I said get lost," the tall man said, his shoulders stiffening. But it was the man at the back that she was more interested in. He was looking very uneasy. She saw he was retreating into the cabin. His gaze darted around. He was twitchy and nervous, and his demeanor was very different from the stoic calmness of the others.

"What's your name?" she asked again. If this situation was pressured, she was ready to take it to the boil.

"It's none of your business. I'm not a killer, but I don't like the police. You guys are corrupt. Now get off our property."

The man at the back was looking even more uncomfortable. She had to push this and see if she could reach a breaking point.

"Hey, you at the back." His head shot up. "Yes, you. You're looking scared. How long have you been here?" she asked him.

The tallest man stepped forward. He looked threatening. As if he was trying to protect his friend and drive her away.

"You're wasting your time, lady," the tall man said. "He's been here a while and he's not the guy you're looking for. Go aggravate someone else. We're done with you."

He turned around and went back inside. His two friends followed him.

Katie strode to the door.

She looked at the twitchy man. He was big and muscular. His shoulders were bulky, and he had a thick neck and powerful arms. The other men were taller than him, but he had the broadest shoulders.

"Your name, sir?" she pressured him again. "Where do you live? How long have you been here today?"

"None of your business," he said, but the tension crackled in his voice.

"Get out," the leader growled. "We got nothing to say to you."

Her focus whipped back to the shifty-eyed man, triggered by a sudden movement he made.

In a flash, Katie read his body language. This had gone beyond threats. The guy was going to grab his gun.

Furious, Katie drew her own gun. She stepped back, out of arm's reach of his friends, and pointed it at him just as he raised his.

Even in the arctic cold, the air seemed to sizzle with tension. Within a moment, they had reached a stand-off.

"Take it easy, Chad," one of the others muttered. So now she knew his name.

"Chad, put your gun down," Katie said with all the force she could muster. This situation had escalated suddenly. Too suddenly. It was dangerous and could explode at any moment. Now she had to contain it.

His hands were shaking. She couldn't tell if it was from anger or bravado. He took a step toward her.

"Put your gun down," Katie said again.

Chad sneered at her. "What you going to do, lady? Shoot me? I'll shoot you first."

Katie knew she was going to have to bluff her way out of this. She had an idea.

"Okay. I'll put my gun down."

Slowly, making no sudden movements, she lowered her service weapon and holstered it again. For a moment she looked into the dark eye of Chad's rifle. Then, unsteadily, he lowered it, too.

The minute that rifle was no longer aimed at Katie, she leaped forward and jumped Chad.

Katie grabbed Chad's rifle and yanked it away, spinning it round so that the barrel was pointing down to the floor. It was heavy. She was fighting for control of it, but she managed to push it away from her.

Chad tried to grab the rifle back, but Katie was too fast for him. She smacked the butt of the gun into his face, and he cried out in pain. He let go the rifle and Katie kicked it back. It wasn't enough to disarm him. Now she had to take him down.

She attacked him, quickly and efficiently, using the brutal takedown tactics she'd learned during her FBI agent training.

They went down on the floor in a tangle of limbs and curses. Chad was trying to hit her, to scratch and punch her. She kept out of his reach, and then she delivered a savage kick to his left knee, one that caused him to howl in pain.

Now he was face down, and she was pinning him there.

"No way," he muttered thickly. "No way."

Twisting around, he lunged at her again.

She punched him in the solar plexus, ducking to avoid his blow. Hers landed squarely. He began coughing and spluttering, badly winded, a spent force for the moment.

Katie stood up. She pulled the cuffs from off her belt. She pulled Chad's arms behind him, then snapped the cuffs around his wrists.

"You're under arrest," she told him. "We're bringing you in on suspicion of the murder of Frances Fick, and others."

CHAPTER TWENTY SIX

Leblanc headed along the trail. His worried thoughts kept returning to Katie, and he had to drag his focus back to his environment.

Was she okay? How was she doing?

He realized he didn't feel competitive against her anymore. Just solving this case would be the biggest win. The sight of that body, laid out on the ice, had filled him with horror and anger. How was it possible someone could be taking these women's lives, so sadistically, just because of what they looked like and represented to him?

The light was fading fast and Leblanc was getting nervous.

This place was too lonely. There was no one around. He couldn't see anyone. He hoped he'd get back to civilization before it got dark.

He could imagine facing the killer. He could imagine his strength, his power, his savagery. Was this what it was like to go over to the dark side? Did the rage take over and turn you into a killing machine?

Leblanc knew the answer. He had seen it in the faces of many killers. There was a darkness inside this man. He wished he knew more about the reasons for why he had become this way. Perhaps the potential had been there from the start, and there had been something that had triggered it.

Often, Leblanc wondered whether the killers he had arrested might have led innocent lives if their circumstances had been slightly different.

He took a deep breath and shook his head, trying to clear it of these thoughts. At this time, he had to remain focused and in control.

"Come on, come on," he muttered.

He needed to concentrate on any sign of the killer's distinctive sole tread in the icy ground. And he needed to be aware of any threat from the frigid woods surrounding him.

He looked quickly right, left, up, and down. The pines were towering above him, the snow beneath his feet was untouched and crisp, the trees all around him were still and silent.

Leblanc gathered all the information he could from his surroundings, and then he pushed it from his mind. He had to focus on the trail ahead, on any sign of the killer. As he walked, he was searching all around him. He made sure to keep his eyes wide open and his senses alert.

He sensed a hint of movement to his right, out at the very edge of his vision. Stopping immediately, he held stock still, and he waited for any sign, for any more movement.

Nothing. He let out a deep breath. The lake and the woods were as spooky as hell today.

Leblanc looked around him once more. He was blindsided by the sheer size of the woods, and by the heavy blanket of snow that muted all the sounds.

Feeling a strange shudder in the ground, he listened hard, and what he heard was a truck. It was coming from the northeast, rattling noisily through the frozen woods. It was a big four-by-four, its engine stirring up the snow.

He stood still, waiting, but the engine faded out of earshot. Where had it come from? The track had to end somewhere, didn't it? It must come to some sort of trailhead or road and from the sound, he would find it soon. He walked on, and as he had guessed, over the next hill, he saw the track ended in a trailhead.

Stumbling through the snow, Leblanc saw the crisscrossed tracks of trucks and snowmobilcs heading away - some to the hills, and the heavier tracks in the direction of the main road. He could hear it though, not see it.

He stood perfectly still, listening to the sound of the breeze in the treetops. He could hear the crunch of the snowflakes beneath his feet, and the groan of the pine trees and the faint swishing of the cars on the road. Everything else was muffled.

But staring down at the tracks gave him an idea. There were tracks from four-by-fours and snowmobiles, but also from an ATV. And there were tire tracks from a truck like the one that had just passed him by.

If the killer lived off the grid in this remote and icy area, he would need a specialized vehicle to drive through the snow and ice. He must have left it somewhere, and perhaps this was why he had come this way, to pick it up. Even though it was just a theory, there was a way he could narrow it down.

There had been several tire tracks near one of the murder scenes. It had been the third murder, he recalled. They had been crisscrossed in the snow nearby. They'd photographed them but had not been able to track their direction due to the heavy snowfall.

Now, he could see if there was any comparison, but he would need to be fast, because it was already snowing again.

He could hear the wind whispering in the trees, and the rattle of the branches as the snowflakes fell.

Picking up his phone, Leblanc called the local precinct - remembering with a sigh that they had bungled Gaby's murder.

"How can I help?" Luckily, Leblanc was speaking to the cooperative officer who had helped him last time.

"I need crime scene photos. There were tire tracks in a few of the pics, and I want to compare them with the ones I'm looking at now," he explained.

"I'll send them now."

Shifting from foot to foot and wishing there was somewhere sheltered to wait, Leblanc hoped that in this case 'now' really did mean 'now.'

It was only a minute later, although it seemed an eternity out there in the cold, that his phone buzzed. He looked at the screen.

Staring from one to the other, Leblanc saw they were very clear. The tire tracks were visible in the snow. There was one set with the exact same tread pattern that he was looking at now.

He felt a surge of excitement and then tried to manage his expectations by reminding himself that snowmobiles were common enough vehicles and that similar models were likely to have the same tires. However he had certainly narrowed his options down to make sure he pursued the right lead.

His phone rang again.

"Did you get them?" the officer asked.

Feeling she should be promoted to detective, Leblanc said, "Thank you very much."

"Do any of them match?"

Leblanc was still staring at the ice tracks on his screen.

He nodded. "I think so," he said.

One of the tracks here had a distinctive chip out of the tread. He thought he could see it in the original crime scene photo also. Leblanc stared down at it, enlarging it, his eyes straining to make out the details.

"I'm going to follow a lead. It's a long shot, though."

"Well. Good luck."

Determinedly, Leblanc set off into the snow.

As soon as he crested the hill, he saw he was right. The tracks led into the wood, and just a hundred yards ahead, he saw a cabin in the distance. The tracks curved around behind it and then disappeared, so Leblanc assumed this man had parked the vehicle behind the cabin.

Leblanc drew his handgun. If he was approaching the killer, he knew the man was armed and dangerous. He would need the element of surprise, to hammer on his door while he was trapped inside.

He brushed his way past a snow-covered branch and jumped as it creaked, and then crashed to the ground, broken by the weight of snow.

Was that a figure ahead? He thought he'd seen a dark-clad man for a moment, but it was gloomy in these woods and his eyes could be playing tricks on him.

The next moment, he flinched as an explosion shattered the silence. Snow showered from a tree to his right. An enraged roar ricocheted through the quiet woods.

As Leblanc dived for cover, plunging behind the tree to his left, his shocked brain pieced together what had happened.

The man at the cabin had seen him and he was shooting. He had a high-caliber rifle and he was a damned accurate shot. Leblanc was still out of range with his handgun, and couldn't return fire.

The situation had just turned deadly.

CHAPTER TWENTY SEVEN

The watcher paced from wall to wall in his cabin hideaway. The place that had always been a peaceful retreat now felt like a prison. The four log walls were closing in. The smoky, wood-infused air felt suffocating.

He felt panicked because he had been seen.

He had made a mistake. He had made it in the stress of the moment, when the woman had tried to run, but he had made it.

Now, he couldn't believe it. How could he have been so stupid?

He'd drawn attention to himself in broad daylight and then he had been caught, after making bad decisions. Fear had taken control and he'd lost all his logic. He'd tried to chase down the witness but he had gotten away.

The cabin was his world. The woods were his refuge.

He felt like a wild animal caught in a trap.

Drawing in a deep breath, he knew he had to leave. It would be better to escape the area completely, even though it was his home. He'd thought his dwelling to be safe and secret but it wouldn't be for long.

There was snow, now. Perhaps that gave him some time. But, as the snow fell, the watcher felt the panic rising in him like a tidal wave.

No. No. He had to do something. He couldn't let the situation overwhelm him. He had to decide.

He paced faster, trying to work out what to do next, but he couldn't think straight. Should he run or hide? Which would work?

At any moment, he expected the cops would kick down the door, even though he'd bolted it from the inside and he hadn't lit the fire in case the smoke clued them up that this cabin was occupied.

Flinching, he saw a shadow moving at the window. But looking again, he realized that perhaps it was just the shadows of the trees as the sun dipped behind the hills. Or perhaps it was just the darkening of the sky as the clouds rolled in.

But he couldn't stop himself from feeling that it was much more than that.

Someone was coming to get him.

Then he heard a voice, and froze.

It was a voice from within. It was coming from inside his own head. It was both his voice and someone else's. It was taunting him, like the voice of a demon.

“You're trapped. There is no escape. You've got no way out.”

And then, the flashbacks started. There was no warning. He just suddenly remembered.

He was six years old. He was playing hide and seek with his older sister, Tanya. His parents were away on a trip to town and they'd gotten snowed in, so it was just the two of them in that old lakeside cottage.

He climbed into her closet. Hiding there, waiting in the dark, he’d heard her call his name. "I'm coming to find you. Ready or not!”

He remembered feeling proud of himself for hiding in his sister's room. She had never looked in there before. But as she walked into the bedroom, Tanya’s voice had changed. It had become low and menacing, a soft whisper.

"I know you went into my room, little brother. I told you never to do that. I told you! I told you!"

He swallowed down fear. This didn’t sound like his sister anymore She sounded different. She was walking toward him. He heard her footsteps on the wooden floor. He could see the shadow coming closer.

He was afraid. He was alone. He was small and he was hiding in the closet.

Her shadow was getting bigger through the tiny crack in the closet door.

She wrenched the door open and grabbed him by the arm, pulled him out of the closet and began to beat him with her fists.

"I told you never to go in my room. I told you never to go in there. Why did you do it?"

He had no idea why he had done it, why he had disobeyed her. He couldn’t tell her why he had gone in there.

Her fists struck him, one, two, three, hard blows. He tried to scream, but she locked his jaw in cruel fingers and forced it closed.

He'd stared up at her, helpless in her grasp, because she might be a girl but she was five years older than him. She was taller and stronger, with her wiry, slim limbs and cruel fingers. Her blue eyes had blazed down at him. She'd shaken her blond hair back impatiently as she held him captive.

"You're a bad, bad boy," she said, raising her hand as she spoke.

Something shifted in her face. She looked like a stranger. She grabbed him by the arm and dragged him from the room. He was frightened but he couldn't stop himself from asking why. He was crying and begging for an answer, but she didn't answer, just gripped him harder, pulling him along behind her.

"Where are we going?" he'd asked.

She didn't answer.

"Where are we going?" he'd asked again, as she dragged him along a dark passage to the kitchen.

"I told you never to go in my room. Why did you do it?" she'd said.

She'd opened the cellar door, the place he hated the most, dark and damp and freezing cold.

"I'm going to teach you a lesson, little brother."

"Please don't make me go in there," he begged.

But she didn't listen. She made him go down. He couldn't stop her.

She'd pushed him down the steps. He'd stumbled, still begging her to tell him why, and she'd followed him down the stairs with a flashlight. He could see the light dancing on the stone walls above him as she shone it in his face.

"You're evil!"

The torch beam was blinding him, hurting his eyes, making the darkness worse.

"You shouldn't have done it."

She'd shone it in his face. He'd tried to hide from the light, squeezing his eyes shut.

"You shouldn't have done it."

He couldn't breathe. He heard himself whimpering.

She locked the door behind her. He heard the key turn in the lock.

He was alone, in the dark and in the cold, on the damp, stone floor, his body trembling and his heart beating frantically.

He'd been terrified. He'd been so frightened that he'd been sick. All he could do was lie there, trembling and sobbing and feeling the agony of being alone and afraid.

He'd never imagined that his sister could be so cruel. She had left him alone in the dark and in the cold, shaking and sobbing, for a long time; he couldn't tell how long. In the cellar, he'd stared up at the blackness of the ceiling and the raw brick walls. The floor had been covered in mud and cobwebs.

He could still feel the spiders scuttling over him.

He'd been starving and hungry down there. The hunger had gnawed at him for all that long night. There was nothing to eat in the cellar. It was a place used only to store empty bottles and junk.

"Why don't you come and let me out? Can you hear me here? Have you forgotten me?" he had called in despair, knowing he was invisible to her.

In the gloom, he'd found a wooden box and had opened it, wondering if it might contain food or candy. But to his disappointment, all it contained was an old chess set. He'd held the pieces, felt their shape in the dark, stroked his fingers over them. Strangely, they had brought him some comfort.

He'd stayed prisoner there until his mother and father had returned. And then, as he'd huddled, despairingly in the darkness, the door above had opened.

"Mom and Dad are back," she had whispered.

She put her finger to her lips, in a gesture so exaggerated that it was comical.

"Swear," she said. "Swear that you won't tell. On your life."

He was never to tell anyone. Ever. He was to keep his secret for her.

He could still hear her voice. It was dark and threatening. Of course he'd obeyed her. He'd never told on her.

But the next time their parents had gone away, she'd done it again. Every time they left, she'd done the same. She'd thrown him into the cellar to be alone, to be punished. And then his parents had died, and he had been hers forever.

The watcher realized he'd wrapped his arms around himself and was rocking back and forth. The cabin was icy cold. The cold and the fear were reminding him of being in the cellar and it was then he knew what he had to do.

He had to kill her, one last time.

He had to go into town. Perhaps she would be there and he could find her again.

She wouldn't be able to come back this time. He would do it right. This time she would not haunt his nightmares and his memories.

He would use the most powerful piece of all, the one he'd been saving in case the others didn't work.

The queen.

Feeling suddenly calm and purposeful, the killer stood up and walked to the door.

CHAPTER TWENTY EIGHT

Katie led the way into the police station, followed by the arresting officer who had met her outside. He was gripping Chad's arm firmly. Chad looked angry and rebellious. Katie was glad he was cuffed. If he hadn't been, she was sure he would have tried to get away.

"Right, Chad, let's go into the interview room and we'll talk about this," the arresting officer said. "We've got a lot of questions."

"Like I'm going to answer any questions," Chad said. "You're arresting me for a crime? I'm no criminal."

"We'll see about that," the officer said.

"I want a lawyer," Chad demanded. "I have rights!" he added querulously.

The officer nodded. "I'm sure you do. Let's go in and we'll talk about it."

While the officer hustled Chad through to the station's single, small side office that doubled as an interview room, Katie walked over to the helpful sergeant at the desk.

"Chad McMasters. Does he have a criminal record?" she asked. "What did you find on him?"

"He does," the sergeant said, after a quick look at the computer screen. "He's got a history. He's done time for assault and battery. And he's a wanted man at this point. He's got an outstanding warrant for his arrest after beating a girlfriend so bad she ended up in the hospital."

"Thanks," said Katie.

She felt encouraged. This was a violent man who took his temper out on women. Assault was a serious crime. It didn't take much to cross over into murder. Physically, Chad checked all the boxes they were looking for. He was strong. His feet were a size eleven. The officer had checked his boots.

The tread pattern on these boots was identical. However, Katie acknowledged that they were a common type of winter boot, sold at most of the general stores nearby. So that alone would not be enough. She needed to get a confession out of him.

Katie took a deep breath, preparing herself. Then she walked into the interview room.

Cuffed to his chair, Chad glared at her. His eyes blazed with hostility. He was a big, muscular man. With his jacket now removed and wearing only a dirty plaid shirt, she saw his forearms were covered in tattoos.

"The recording apparatus is working. He's all yours. I'll be listening in," the arresting officer said to her quietly. Then he left her to it and closed the door.

She sat in the corner of the room, and looked thoughtfully at Chad McMasters. He glared back at her in anger.

"Why were you going to shoot me?" she said.

"I was bluffing," Chad protested. "I'm innocent. Whatever you think I did, I didn't do it!"

Katie stared him down.

"If you want to tell your side of the story, you're going to have to do better than this. This isn't going to work. The tread of your boots matches with what we found at the crime scene. You were there, weren't you?"

"You've got nothing on me," Chad insisted.

"What about your record? You've beaten women before. We checked. We have testimony. This is a serious charge. This is murder. Where were you this morning? Where were you last night? If you didn't do it then prove it to me."

Chad stared at her, breathing hard, flexing his hands and clenching his fists. She saw his muscles ripple in his forearm.

"Look, lady, I don't have to prove nuthin'. You're the one who arrested me. I want my lawyer. Let him prove it."

"What time did you get up this morning?" Katie said. "Where did you go, last night and this morning?"

"What time do you think?" Chad sneered. "Are you the time police?"

"In your past, you've been violent to women. You've got an anger management problem, Chad. You have a history of violence," Katie said. "We can put you away for a very long time. I can get a confession out of you. I've got you dead to rights. Unless you tell me. Where were you this morning? Where were you last night? That's all I need. The rest will sort itself out."

Chad pressed his lips together. Finally, she saw that the reality of his situation was sinking in.

His eyes lit up.

“Look here, lady. If I tell you where I was, and it wasn’t the murder, will you keep me out of trouble for it?”

Katie thought.

“That depends. If you’re truthful and you help me, I’ll do my best.”

Chad hesitated. She could see this was a tipping point. He was either going to decide to talk, or else, he would shut down and refuse to say another word.

Katie stayed quiet, letting him think through the consequences of each for himself. Pressuring him might cause him to retreat. She needed to invite him to fill the silence with his words.

To her extreme relief, he began talking.

"I was doing a deal last night," he muttered. “I did pass by the area you mentioned earlier. I’d been to a diner and was heading back to the lodge.”

"A deal? What kind of deal?"

He looked down, scowling at the floor.

"Guns. Ammunition. I've got some ex-militia contacts who live in the woods. They buy gear from me. I get it from someone else. They need to protect themselves," he insisted defiantly.

"Can you prove it?" she asked, but Chad had the wrong end of the stick.

"If I want to sell guns and ammo, I can do it,” he ranted. “I don't need a license. I'm no criminal. I'm a businessman, okay? I'm a gun dealer. I'm a patriot. You have no right to stop me. Everyone needs to defend themselves. Their families. People out here, they need to look after their families. We're close-knit in this area. We protect each other."

For some reason, what Chad said was making Katie feel as if she'd almost had an important insight into the killer. Unfortunately the key word was 'almost.' Whatever the connection had been, it had been too fleeting for her to grasp.

"Okay, Chad. That's fine. I understand your reasons. What time do you think it was when you left home to go work last night? What time did you leave?"

"I left at six. It took me an hour to get there on the snowmobile. My contact met me at a place near the border. That's where we stash the guns and ammo away. There’s a bar about half an hour away, on the main road. I was there from seven until eight, when he arrived. They know me. They can confirm I was there. The waitresses at the diner will tell you I went there this morning and wasn’t killing nobody."

"You say the guns are still there?"

"Yes. I left them there last night. Tonight, I'm due to go back and meet the seller."

"Give us the name of your supplier. And you'll need to show us on a map where the bar and diner are. We're going to check your alibi."

Chad stared at her stonily.

And then he nodded. "Okay," he snapped.

Straight away, Katie stood up and left the room.

"Did you get that?" she asked the officer, who was hurrying toward her.

"I got it all," he confirmed. "We'll follow up on the lead and we'll put a sting operation into place for tonight. We'll try put a stop to this."

"Thanks," Katie said. "Don't press charges on him. Not for that, anyway. Let's keep our side of the deal. We might need him again someday."

She headed out, feeling deeply disappointed. Chad wasn't the killer. This was a dead end.

Katie didn't know where to turn next and frustratingly, she couldn't get back that spark of insight she'd had.

Was there a way she could go back to it?

Pacing the police station's lobby, Katie relooked at her thought process, remembering the other serial crimes she'd solved, and what their patterns had been. These crimes seemed random and unpredictable, but they were not random to the killer. There was usually a trigger, a motive, a reason.

The chess pieces provided a connection and a clue. The cycle was speeding up, meaning higher levels of anger or desperation.

He was angry, Katie decided. He was killing someone that the blonde women represented, and he was doing so again and again. That was the key. It lay in what they meant to him. And she needed to work out why he felt the urgent and increasing need to do this.

At that moment, her phone rang.

Quickly, she grabbed it, seeing it was Leblanc on the line.

"I need help," he said, sounding tense and speaking rapidly. "I followed snowmobile tracks down to a cabin in the woods. There's a guy in there, but he's shot at me. High-caliber weapon. I've taken cover but I need backup, fast."

Her adrenaline surged. Her partner was in danger and could even now be cornered by the killer.

"Send me the coordinates." Katie rushed to her car as she spoke. "I'm on my way."

CHAPTER TWENTY NINE

Leblanc killed the call, shoving his phone back in his pocket, trying to do it all while behind the cover of the trees.

He hoped the man in the woods hadn't heard his muttered words.

He didn't dare to move, even though he was shuddering with cold. He'd managed to move to thicker cover about ten minutes ago but he was unable to leave the woods without walking through the open and into the rifle's sights. Now, stillness and silence were his only hope for survival.

From beyond, near the wooden cabin where the snowmobile tracks had led, he could hear the man's angry cries.

"I know you're out there! I'm going to find you. You're targeting me; I can tell!"

The man was cursing and shouting. He didn't know how close Leblanc was to him or where he was.

He knew it was deeply ironic that he'd been worried about Katie coming up against a paranoid survivalist, and then he was the one who'd walked straight into the madhouse.

Although he couldn't get away, he knew if he stayed in this thicket, the man would eventually find him.

He had the corner of the cabin between himself and the man. He could make a dash for it, duck behind the building, then try to escape.

He didn't want to do it, though, but time was running out.

Suddenly, he heard a sound that froze his heart. Footsteps, crunching through the snow.

"Don't try to run away," the man shouted. "I know you're out there. I'm going to track you down and kill you. You, and any other cop who gets in my way!"

He sounded genuinely psychotic. Also, he was sounding closer. He'd finally found Leblanc's hiding place.

With an explosion, he fired his rifle and Leblanc cringed down.

Branches crashed above him as the bullet sped past. Leaves and twigs showered down. Flattening himself, he kept as low as he could.

"I'm going to get you!"

Leblanc didn't dare to move. The man fired again.

Leblanc's breath caught in his throat.

He took a moment to think and then he called out, "You do not want to hurt anybody. You're angry. You are confused. You need to talk to me. If we talk face to face, you can tell me what's happened and let me help you. I'm your only hope. I'm your only way out."

The response was almost immediate and Leblanc was sure he was in real danger.

A bullet thudded into the snow near his feet and he felt the ground shudder.

"I'm not afraid of you. I'm not afraid of you, you hear!"

The seconds were ticking down. He'd have to take his chances with the handgun. He must be close enough now for Leblanc to return fire. Bracing himself, he got ready to leap out and face him down.

And then, he heard the whiplash crack of another gunshot and the man shouted again. But this time, Leblanc was astonished to hear shock and pain in his voice.

"You hit me! You hurt me!" the man roared.

"Leblanc!"

Relief flooded him as he heard his partner's voice. Just in time, Katie had arrived.

Leblanc burst out from behind thc tree, his gun at the ready.

"Drop your weapon," Leblanc shouted to the survivalist.

"Drop it!" Katie roared at the same time.

The man looked back and forth between them, his face pale and sweating.

"Drop it!"

He dropped the weapon. He was wincing in pain. Katie had caught him in the shoulder and Leblanc could see blood dripping, bright and red on the white snow.

Sirens blared. Katie must have called police backup before she left, and now they were here. Leblanc didn't dare lower his gun, though. Not even a fraction. He waited and watched as the two officers jumped out of the car and ran heavily through the snow toward them.

The man, who looked in his thirties, with curly brown hair and a thin, unshaven face, lowered himself to the snowy ground. His face was white, his lips were quivering and he was bent over, holding his shoulder where the bullet had gone through.

"Take me to the hospital! You shot me!" he said, as the police hauled him to his feet.

Only then did Katie lower her gun.

She walked over to Leblanc, her footsteps scrunching in the snow.

"Are you okay?" she asked anxiously.

"Cold, but not hurt," Leblanc admitted, stamping his feet to get the circulation back, and feeling thankful this ordeal was over.

"Let's take a look inside his cabin," she said. "We might find something there to help us. Earlier, I thought about what is triggering the killer. We need to look for what's making him so angry and obsessed. We need some evidence that ties his mindset in with these crimes."

"Good idea."

Leblanc strode to the small cabin behind her.

The man clearly lived alone. In the cabin, there was very little. He had a bed. A table with two chairs. An old fireplace with a fire that had gone out and was cold. There was only one item that looked out of place, and that was a Polaroid camera on the table.

"I haven't seen one of those for years," Leblanc said, moving over to take a look.

His gaze sharpened as he saw there were photos scattered on the desk.

"Look!" Leblanc said, pointing. He stared down in shock.

The photos were of women. They seemed to have been taken randomly. Women walking in town. Women helping customers inside shop windows. A woman hiking, her hair covered by a pink hat. The shots weren't clear. They were blurry and the angles were bad, as if the man had taken them discreetly, while trying to keep out of sight.

He felt excitement swell inside him. This man was a stalker. Had he moved on and taken the next step to killing his prey?

This evidence changed everything. It showed preplanning, that he was a stalker who had watched his prey before attacking.

Now all that remained was joining the dots, the hows and whys, linking the pieces of evidence together. Hopefully he would confess.

"I'm just glad we got him at last," he said.

But to his surprise, he saw Katie didn't look as convinced as he felt.

"Where are the chess pieces?" she asked, looking around the cabin. "There's no sign of the most important evidence we need."

"Perhaps they're hidden, and they'll find them in the search. Or they might even be on his person. We'd better get going," Leblanc said.

She seemed unsure, lagging behind him. When they reached the car she hung back. She looked back into the woods, frowning, as if she was doubting herself and the entire chain of events that had led them to this moment.

Leblanc turned to her, his blood chilling. "Katie?"

She was staring at the cabin, her blue eyes narrowed.

"Something's not adding up," she said. The words made his shiver.

She was staring, almost as if she was looking right through the cabin and into the trees behind it.

"I'm not sure about this," she murmured to him. "I've been trying and trying to get inside his mind, but looking at those photos still doesn't give me enough of a reason to join the dots. Not in the way I was hoping for. Leblanc, I know the evidence is pointing his way, but I feel certain we're missing something."

CHAPTER THIRTY

Samantha Hamish walked out of the computer store where she'd helped her last customer of the day. She'd made some good sales. She was looking forward to the commission report at month-end. Even though all her colleagues joked it was easy for her to sell, because she was blonde and slim and blue-eyed, Samantha and her boss, knew it was because she was very service-oriented and knowledgeable about the products.

She loved to help people. Sales is always about helping people. That was what she'd taken to heart in her training, even though this job was only a stepping stone. When she'd completed her computer science degree, she wanted to become a programmer and write software to help people. She had so many ideas.

She said goodbye to her boss and headed out the door.

It was late in the afternoon and the light was already gone. It was a gray, somber day and extremely cold. She could feel the cold burning her cheeks as she hustled across the parking lot.

She was eager to get home to her husband. They would make dinner together. She wasn't a great cook but she enjoyed the process. Quality time.

Home was a ten-minute drive away and although the snow was starting to fall again, she knew she'd get home safely as the roads were clear.

She'd just climbed into her car when she saw the man waving at her.

He was walking toward her, looking purposeful yet apologetic. And cold. Wrapped up in a heavy coat, she couldn't see anything beyond that he was tall and pale skinned, with red blooms in his lean cheeks from the cold. She thought she recognized him and had seen him before locally.

"Hey there! Are you heading down Main Street? I'm in need of a hand."

"A hand?" she said, puzzled.

"I'm out of gas. My snowmobile ran out and my phone isn't charging. I just need to get as far as my brother's place, corner Main and Aster, on the road to the lake."

"I'm sorry, I can't help you." Samantha felt bad to refuse, but rules were rules, and strangers were strangers.

She started the car, but he tapped on the window pleadingly. He did look very cold, she saw.

"Wait," he said. "I don't want you to think I'm a psycho or something. I'm not that kind of person. I live near here. I'm just in trouble and I need a hand. I'll pay you for the ride."

He took out a ten dollar bill.

It wasn't the money that convinced her so much as the need to be kind, to help. That came naturally to her, Samantha acknowledged. The money was proof that he was a decent guy and she'd been wrong to mistrust him.

"Okay," she said. "I can take you that far."

She unlocked the doors and he hurried around and got in the passenger side.

She'd been taught never to get into a car alone with a stranger, especially a man. But he was freezing out there, she thought. He really must be in trouble.

"Here you are." He placed the ten dollar bill in the car's cubbyhole. "Thank you."

Samantha tried to relax as they drove because it didn't seem he wanted to make conversation along the way. She tried to enjoy the music on her playlist, while keeping focused on the snowy, icy road.

"You need to be careful," he told her suddenly. "I hear there's been some problems in the area."

She felt a jolt of fear.

"I know," she said. "I've heard that, too."

She glanced at him, suddenly distrustful. Had she really seen him around? Or was he a stranger?

Suddenly, she wished she hadn't offered to give him a ride at all.

She got all the way to the end of Main and then glanced at him expectantly. Her heart accelerated as he looked back at her.

She unlocked the car, willing him to get out and for this whole situation not to turn weird, or dangerous.

"You really need to be careful," he said. "Listen, if you want me to help you any time, I will. We all need to keep each other safe now. Thanks for the ride."

To her utter relief, he got out of the car.

He hadn't been a psycho. He'd been a regular local guy and in fact he'd looked out for her. Nothing had been wrong.

She watched him walk into the two-story apartment block, making sure he was safe inside.

The door closed behind him.

She let out a long, deep breath.

But then, her car's back door was wrenched open, letting in a blast of cold air.

She screamed as another man in a heavy overcoat jumped inside.

"I have a gun," he told her, sounding urgent and aggressive and unhinged. "Don't turn the car around. I need you. I can see you're heading in the right direction. Out to the lake. Don't run. Don't scream again. Just drive."

"No," Samantha whispered. This couldn't be happening to her. Thanks to her kindheartedness, she'd landed in the nightmare she'd dreaded. She'd been unaware and distracted with her doors unlocked. This man had seen an opportunity and he'd taken it.

She could feel the gun barrel cold against her neck. Above her fear, which was huge, she felt a thread of resolve that she had to get out of this alive.

Shakily, she drove on. They were heading out of town now. The road was deep in snow. The car jolted and rocked as it drove. She had to think what to do. Could she call her husband? She feared that if she tried, he would shoot.

"Tanya," he said and she let out a breath of horror, because this guy was delusional. He thought he was someone else.

"That - that's not me," she stammered.

"Tanya!" he said again, angrily.

She checked behind her. Town was out of sight.

"Stop the car. We're getting out," he said.

This was her only chance. Somehow, she had to distract him and she came up with the only, desperate plan she could think of.

"If you want the car, take the keys."

She tugged them from the ignition and flung them into the back of the car.

Instinctively, he followed their movement. In that moment, hoping he was distracted and wouldn't shoot, Samantha wrenched open the door and leaped out.

“Hey!” she heard his voice, angry and shocked, but didn’t even hesitate. She ran, panic-stricken, through the snow, needing to get away from the road, away from where he could drive after her. She had no idea where she was heading.

"I'm coming for you, Tanya!" she heard him again, now furious, the sharp words crackling through the air behind her. "Coming, ready or not!"

She didn't dare look around. All she could do was run. But there was no sign of where she was or where she was going.

The snow burned her cheeks.

Here, in this frozen landscape, Samantha had to confront the knowledge that no one knew where she was. She was isolated, alone. There was nobody who could help her. Even the hunters and fishermen had retreated inside, sheltering from the storm.

Even more terrifying than being alone in the snow was the realization that he was going to hunt her down. She'd be easy prey.

The cold was spreading through her. She felt it burn her feet. She'd been so intent on escaping that she'd forgotten she was wearing her red patent leather boots. In the shop, they were perfect. But out here, she couldn't feel her feet anymore.

She'd only had on a light coat. Already, her arms were numb and she was shuddering with cold despite her panicked flight.

If she could not find shelter she would die. That grim, terrible reality descended on her. She was totally disoriented. She had no idea where she was. Snowbanks loomed in all directions.

And there was the cold, worsening with every moment, clamping down on her like a vise. It was slowing her, chilling her through to the bone.

She had to find a place to hide. She'd left her phone in her purse, and her purse in the back seat of her car. She couldn't call for help and was terrified to shout at all, because she knew he was still coming for her. Would he find her?

She ran, stumbling through the snow, realizing that this was it. If he didn't kill her, the cold would. She couldn't carry on much longer.

Then, looming ahead of her through the fluttering snow, she saw a cabin. It was a simple wooden structure, small and isolated from the road. It looked empty.

She ran up to the door and pounded on it, wildly.

"Help me! Please! Help me!"

Impulsively, now shaking with cold, she tried the door and to her shock, it opened, the hinges creaking.

Samantha flung herself inside and slammed the door, hoping he hadn't seen which way she went. Hoping she'd be safe here and he wouldn't find her, because if he did find her, she would be trapped inside.

She waited. The only sound was the rushing of her terrified breath. She was shuddering with cold and fear. Had he been able to follow her tracks? He seemed like a person who would do that.

Again she heard his voice. “Ready or not!” but thanks to the gusting wind, she couldn’t tell how close he was or even where it was coming from.

But she knew he was hunting her. This tiny shack was the only building she’d seen in the white-out. It was inevitable that he would find her soon.

CHAPTER THIRTY ONE

Standing outside the hospital ward, with a police guard stationed at the door, Katie felt conflicted. Logically, she knew this should be the killer inside.

His name was Jack Cross. He had a record for housebreaking and assault. He'd been released from prison two years ago and since his parole, had gone off the grid. A hunter. A fisherman. In every way, this fitted the profile. He had a history of crime, he had shot at law enforcement, and he had photos of women in his cabin.

And yet, she was certain that there was a piece of the puzzle missing. Not all the photos in the cabin had been of blondes. There were some of redheads, some of brunettes, some of older women. And the initial police search had not uncovered any chess pieces, either in the cabin, in his vehicles, or on his person. Not even any sign of woodworking tools.

"Has he said anything so far?" she asked the police officer.

" Johnson and Anderson did an initial debrief when he was brought in. They said he was obstructive. He spoke a bit, but I'm not sure how much sense he made. Leblanc is in there now," the man replied. "Johnson and Anderson are going out there to speak to his neighbors and see if anyone saw or heard snowmobiles at night."

"Does he seem to know what's going on?"

"You mean is he crazy?" the officer asked.

"I mean, is he aware of his situation?" Katie tried to explain. She felt the killer would be sharp, rather than confused.

"He's very aware. He's just not talking. But I don't think he's crazy, ma'am. I've seen his eyes. He's cold. Calculating. And he's a great deal stronger than he looks."

He glanced through the window into the ward. Katie followed his gaze.

There he was. The hospital gown looked incongruous on his big, muscular shoulders. His left arm was in a sling. His right arm was handcuffed to the bed railing, because they were taking no chances with this dangerous criminal who'd already proven he had no reserves about trying to kill.

Inside, interrogating him, she saw Leblanc. He had a recording device on the table nearby and a notebook in his hand. They'd decided to go in separately and question him, thinking that two approaches might work better and that information gathered in the first interview could be used in the next.

But it seemed Leblanc was done. As she watched, he turned around and walked to the door, looking frustrated.

"What happened?" Katie asked as he stepped out of the room.

"He's a manipulator and a liar," Leblanc said. "He'll try to string you along. Don't be fooled."

Katie felt alarmed. "What did he say?"

Leblanc shrugged. "He talked a lot. Randomly. It was frustrating because he refused to answer my questions. Just rambled on. Then he said he had something to tell me, and I thought he was going to confess to the murders. But he told me that he didn't do anything wrong. He was insistent about it. But not in an anxious way. It felt to me as if he was hiding something, and laughing about it."

As he spoke, the man began to laugh again. It was a deep, rumbling sound and it sent shivers up Katie's spine.

"Let me go in," she said.

She walked in, trying to think about how she could approach him and if it would be possible to crack open this shell of resistance he was hiding behind.

He turned to her.

"It can't be comfortable in here, Mr. Cross. Handcuffed to the rail." She sat down. "There are pain meds waiting for you as soon as we're done here. There's an easier way than this."

He shrugged. Stared at her with cold eyes.

"I know what you're thinking," he said. " You're looking for a murderer and you think I'm your guy."

"Are you?" she asked.

He laughed again. "Think what you want, I know you will. I know you want to find out about me, what I did last night, where I was today, where I went. You want to be absolutely sure that you've got the right guy. But guess what? You'll never be sure. So maybe you'll start to trick me. To force me into saying the things you need from me. I'm not buying that. There's no way I'm going along with it. I'm not saying another word." He closed his mouth firmly.

"Why not?" Katie tried. "What are you scared of? We don't want to arrest the wrong guy. If you're innocent, then just tell us so."

Staring intently at Katie, Cross shook his head. Then he put his head back on the pillow and stared at the ceiling.

"Do you play chess? Do you own a chess set?" she asked.

He shrugged. His expression didn't change.

"We need to know. If you can be cleared it will change everything. For your own future," she tried, but he didn't even twitch.

Feeling she needed a new approach, she got up and walked out.

Leblanc shook his head. "He's being even worse with you. And he's like a different person now, all withdrawn."

"I just don't understand why he's not even talking. He should talk. If he's not our guy, why would he want to make us think he is?"

"He's guilty," Leblanc said. "He's just buying time and taunting us. This is another game to him. Let's get the charges written up and start the process. Do the hard work. DNA. Trace evidence. Measurements. Sole prints. Johnson and Anderson may pick up witness accounts that will incriminate him. If we search the area surrounding the cabin, we might get more evidence, too."

"He's not going to confess," Katie said. "We'll need a lot of evidence if all we have is circumstantial."

Leblanc shook his head. "He was never going to confess to anything. Why would he prove his guilt?"

"You believe he's the killer?" Katie asked.

Leblanc nodded. "Yes, I do."

"I still think we should relook at this. What if we are missing the real killer?" Katie said, feeling agitated.

Leblanc shook his head. "We're under pressure to close this. And this is a dangerous criminal. He's proved that beyond doubt. He fits the profile."

Katie looked back through the window. Jack was laughing again.

There must be something they hadn't considered. But what? They'd looked at all the contacts. They'd identified no links. They'd narrowed down the probabilities.

What hadn't they done?

Standing outside the ward, she felt goose bumps prickle her arms as she realized what they had missed.

"We haven't gone back far enough in old case history. Whoever he is, we can be sure this killer was born and raised in this area. There must be something we can uncover, some evidence, of when he started or what made him who he is."

Leblanc was shaking his head. "We have explored case history. We looked at all the cold cases in the area and found nothing similar."

"How far did you go back?" she asked.

"I think we went as far as five or six years."

Katie shook her head. " We need to go further back. Ten, twenty years. Because whatever happened might have had its roots in this killer's early life. I think that's where all of this started."

*

Arriving at the police station, Katie headed to the back office and found a computer in a quiet corner. There, she brought up the database which contained the cold cases and unsolved murders.

She raced through it, going back years and years, hoping to find what she now thought might be there, hidden in the past.

A murdered woman. A pretty, blonde woman. That would have been the first one, that had set him on this path.

Agonized, her mind flashed back to Josie. Serial killers were patient. They had all the time in the world to follow their deadly agenda.

She scanned the names. Dates. Locations. Tension knotted in her stomach. It was never easy to explore the past.

Forcing herself to breathe slowly and deeply, she kept scanning.

Where was it? Where was the woman who had triggered the killings? Or had her instincts been completely wrong?

She scanned page after page, keeping focused, trying to stay calm even though she was worried her entire line of reasoning had been faulty.

And then she found it.

Gasping in triumph, feeling as if the clock was now ticking down to the very last second, she clicked on the link to the case file and read through it.

The case was from exactly ten years ago, and the victim was Tanya Foxcroft. She'd lived on the shores of the lake in her small family home. And, at the age of twenty-two, she'd been stabbed and left out on the ice. No arrests had ever been made. A couple of suspects had been released after proving alibis. As of today, the murder was still unsolved.

Katie had never worked through a case so fast.

There were still unanswered questions. She didn't know why it had taken ten years for the killer to start up again, but perhaps he had been incarcerated, or institutionalized, or something else traumatic might have happened to trigger him. Perhaps the ten-year anniversary had been significant and brought his demons back. There were lots of possible reasons.

So if this was the first case, who was the killer?

Katie looked again at the case details. And then she saw what she needed to. The one fact that joined the dots.

Tanya's parents had died in a car crash. She had been sixteen at the time, and her younger brother, Caleb, had been put in her care. After that, Caleb had been taken out of school. Child protection services had been called out to the home a few times because shouts and screaming had been heard. Caleb had been a suspect at the time of Tanya's death but they had no solid evidence and had not charged him for the crime. Then, he fell off the radar. He had disappeared.

"I think I know what happened," Katie said.

At that moment, the phone rang. It was Clark on the line, anxiety flaring in his voice.

"We may have a problem," he snapped. "There's a missing person just been called in. Girl named Samantha, who works for a computer store. A coworker saw a stranger climb into the passenger seat of her car, and called her husband to let him know. She still isn't home and they have no idea where she is. Is this just a coincidence? Or a copycat crime? How the hell could this happen? Our suspect's in custody. Is he working with an accomplice?"

Katie stood up.

"Clark, I think we arrested the wrong guy," she said heavily. "I've been researching cold cases and found one that ties up from ten years ago. There's a suspect, Caleb Foxcroft, who lived locally, and we need to find him. If we move fast, we have a chance of saving this woman, but we can't slip up again."

CHAPTER THIRTY TWO

Katie accelerated in the direction of the lake. The SUV fishtailed on the icy road. Her hand light on the wheel, she corrected it. Dread chilled her stomach as she thought about what lay ahead, and what the killer might already have done. They couldn't lose another victim. Not if there was any risk that they had the wrong suspect in custody.

Leblanc was heading into town to track Samantha's car. If he could, he would start the search operation from that side.

And she was racing to the old house where the Foxcrofts had lived, hoping that Caleb might still be living there.

The SUV skidded in the snow and Katie corrected, thinking only of Caleb.

He hadn't gone far, she was sure of it. He would not have gone too far away from his childhood home, where torture or trauma must have shaped him.

Here was the home. Slowing, Katie took a look.

The wooden house at the end of the road was totally unlike what she had expected to see. She'd expected an abandoned ruin, with broken windows the mirror image in her mind of Caleb's mental state.

But this home looked neat and cared for, and there was a red SUV parked outside. It looked bright against the dark sky and looming clouds.

Katie jumped out, ran up to the home, and knocked on the door.

A woman's face appeared behind the glass pane.

"FBI," Katie said. "Can you open up? We're looking for Caleb Foxcroft."

The woman opened the door. "Caleb doesn't live here, anymore, ma'am," she said politely. "We bought the house a few years ago."

She glanced at the sky, looking worried. A gust of wind nearly tore the door out of her hand but she held on.

Katie felt her stomach sink. "Do you know where we can find him?"

The woman started to shake her head, then stopped.

"There's something," she said. "I remember...yes, I do remember he mentioned where he lives. He came here recently and told us as he left.

I'm not surprised you're looking for him. I thought he was a very troubled man, and seemed unstable."

"Why was he here?" Katie asked.

"He wanted something from the cellar."

"From the cellar?" Katie said incredulously. "There were still possessions of theirs in there?"

The woman shook her head. "No, of course not. We cleared it out completely. It was a creepy place, full of junk. We clad it in wood and turned it into a downstairs bar area. But we let him go down there anyway because – well, because he didn't seem quite right in the head," she said kindly.

"What was he looking for?" Katie asked.

"He wanted a chess set. He was very anxious about it. He said it was important to him, and it had been in the cellar, but I couldn't help him. He actually got quite upset. Irrational, you know? At one stage he blamed me and said I was hiding it from him. He said it had been ten years, and the time had come to use it. Eventually I gave him twenty dollars and said he should buy one from the general store in town. To replace the one he lost. He took the money, and then he said in a spiteful way that he would make one."

Katie felt ice flood her spine.

"Do you have any idea where he is now?" she asked.

"Not exactly. He told us he lived a couple of miles to the south, in a cabin out along the lake road. Near a fishing pier. I remember he gave us the directions in detail because he wanted us to bring him the chess set if we found it. I thought I'd do something for him as he didn't seem right in the head. Maybe drop off groceries, or something. But I haven't done that so far. Perhaps when summer comes."

"Thank you," Katie said.

"You mustn't go out that way," the woman said, sounding concerned. "There's been a weather warning. There's a huge snowstorm on the way."

Ignoring her advice, Katie sprinted for her car.

The woman was right. The sky had never seemed more menacing. A freezing wind was blasting in. This was going to be more than just a snowfall. There was a blizzard approaching.

She had to try and get there before the storm hit.

Ice crystals flew up from the tires as Katie accelerated along the road, driving at a speed that even she knew was dangerous.

As she drove, she tried calling Leblanc to let him know that she was on her way. It rang and rang but he didn't answer. She hoped he had managed to locate Samantha's car.

She caught her breath as the snow began to pour down. It fell in a rush, a whirling of flakes that surrounded her, cold and blinding.

Peering through the icy maelstrom, Katie was starting to worry. She couldn't see any sign of a cabin or a fishing pier. Was she going the right way? Or had she missed it as the snowstorm had descended.

She could barely see the road in front of her.

The wind was howling through the trees. Icy shards slammed against the car, rocking it. Katie gripped the wheel, grit her teeth, and kept going. Was she going to make it?

She was moving into a world of total isolation. It felt as if she was fighting her way through a thick and suffocating blanket.

Her wheels spun on the ice and she felt, rather than heard, a thud. The car shuddered once, then stopped.

Filled with despair, she climbed out, fighting through the whirling snow to see what she'd connected with. Hopefully she could somehow get the car away from the obstacle, and going again.

But she never got as far as checking, because as she glanced to the right, she saw it, just as the woman had described, but almost invisible in the snow. A wooden cabin, set out on the lakeside.

Abandoning the car, she set off, fighting through the snow toward it. There was no time for hesitation. She had to assume he was inside, armed and waiting.

She drew her gun. Braced herself. Then flung her left shoulder into the wooden door as she turned the handle.

"FBI!" she screamed.

The door flew open and she was in, her eyes wide in the darkness, her finger tight on the trigger.

But he wasn't there. To her astonishment, the only occupant of the cabin was a terrified looking blonde woman, huddled in the corner, a dirty blanket pulled over her.

"Help me," she pleaded. Her lips were blue with cold. "There's a man chasing me. I got away, but he's following."

"Samantha?" Katie asked quickly.

She nodded, looking surprised.

"He's going to find you here. This is his home. His cabin. We need to get out."

Samantha stood up, staggering. She looked clumsy with cold, and Katie's heart sank as she saw her inadequate gear. This woman would freeze within seconds. What if the car was badly stuck? There was no way she could help move it. It might not be drivable now.

Still, it was a better plan than staying here.

"Come on," she encouraged. Taking off her jacket, she wrapped it around Samantha and grasped her arm. Samantha clearly had no feeling in her feet and Katie had to lean against her to support her.

Katie flung open the door of the cabin and her heart sank as she realized she could no longer see the road. To the right, the lake was hidden in swirling snow, and the left side of the cabin was blocked by the trees.

At that moment, a shape loomed into view. Dark against the whiteness. Tall, threatening. He had a gun aimed directly at Samantha. With the other woman leaning against her, Katie couldn't get her gun around to him in time.

"Who are you?" he asked, glancing at Katie angrily. His voice was rough and harsh.

"FBI," she replied. It felt surreal to be speaking to this murderer. Surreal, and perilous.

""You shouldn't be here. I've come for her. I thought she'd double back to her car. Then I wondered if she'd found her way here. And she did. She came to me. Now leave us."

He spoke rapidly, urgently. He looked at her as if she was nothing more than an obstacle to be removed. His eyes were icy cold and strangely empty. Katie was certain he wouldn't hesitate to shoot.

She did the only thing she could. First, she shoved Samantha behind her into the most protected position she could be. And then, as fast as she could, she attacked him, going for the muzzle of that gun, hoping that surprise would give her an advantage.

Katie flung herself at the hunting rifle, slamming it wide as a shot exploded in the air.

The gun clattered to the floor, dislodged from his grasp. She tried to grab it but he kicked it into the corner. Struggling to gain the advantage in this deadly fight, she fired her gun, but missed. He was attacking her now, going for her gun, his fingers digging into her arm. He was incredibly, insanely strong.

"It's too late," he said, his voice low and hoarse as they struggled. "You're too late."

She struck out with her fist, at the side of his jaw, as hard as she could. She wanted to hit him. Hurt him. Disable him. But he was whip-fast and his other hand lashed around.

Now it was her gun in his vise grip. She had only a second to spare before he forced the barrel around and she was shot with her own weapon.

Desperately, Katie tried her only final plan.

She launched at him with all her strength, hoping she could unbalance him and throw him off his stride before he fired.

But it didn't work. He kicked back at her, his foot slamming against her shoulder. To Katie's horror, the impact numbed her hand and she loosened her grip on the weapon. It clattered to the floor and he kicked it away, leaning down to grab his rifle.

She still had no feeling in her damned arm except for a surge of prickly pain.

Quickly the man stepped back, out of reach. He stood in the corner of the cabin, grinning breathlessly as he raised the hunting rifle. Katie was all out of options as she watched his gloved finger tighten on the trigger. He was going to shoot. But probably not to kill. As he aimed the gun at her leg, she knew that he wanted her to suffer first.

CHAPTER THIRTY THREE

Leblanc fought his way through the snow. He'd managed to track Samantha's car up to where it had been abandoned, but the car had been empty, the keys in the back seat, and no trace of her nearby. Since then he'd been casting around in wider circles, frantic with worry, looking for any sign or sound of her.

He was feeling lost and panicked in the worsening snow. So far, he hadn't found any footsteps or any trace of where she could have gone. It was a critical situation and the snow was working against him, blanketing all trace of the killer.

At the same time, he'd had a strange, uneasy feeling that there was someone else around. He couldn't explain it. Perhaps it was the wailing of the wind playing tricks on him, a sound that was unearthly in its intensity.

That was it, he decided, as Samantha's car came into view again. It was time to go back. He couldn't continue in this white-out. It was getting too dangerous. He'd go back to where he'd left his car and make contact with Winter.

But then, as he walked around the car, he saw tracks.

They weren't the ones he expected to see. And they definitely hadn't been there earlier. These looked fresh, and they were the same large boot prints he recognized from previous scenes.

Confusingly, they seemed to circle up to the car and then head away. The trail was distinct. Most definitely, the prints leading away from the car were newly made.

Had the killer been circling and hunting her, too?

If so, had he found her?

These prints provided the most valuable clue he might get. Even though conditions were getting dangerous, he had to follow them before they were covered by snow.

As fast as he could, scanning the ground, Leblanc set off in pursuit.

The storm was picking up now and progress was difficult. There was a gusty wind and the snow was swishing past him in great waves, obscuring the prints so that the trail was all but invisible. Leblanc struggled to keep moving forward in the whirling whiteness, realizing that the weather was as much his enemy as the killer was.

He had to find him. Before it was too late.

Leblanc began to shiver. He'd been moving forward steadily, but now he could not see any signs of the prints. He was disoriented in the snow.

He felt panic rise. He had no idea where he was, or where the road was. And there was no way to check.

Think, he said. Think. Try to go straight. You'll pick it up again. If not, at least you can try to get closer.

Forcing himself to suppress his anxiety and stay calm, he fought on.

And then, through the screaming wind and blowing snow, he saw the shape of a small, wooden building ahead. This had to be it! It was the only cover he'd seen. She had to be there.

If the killer had been circling the car, perhaps that meant Samantha had run off and he hadn't found her yet, Leblanc thought, with a surge of hope as he surveyed this potential hiding place that represented a chance she might be alive.

What would he find? Would he be too late? He scrambled through the drifting snow, heading for the cabin's door.

The wind swirled with a furious intensity. His lungs felt like they were freezing. His whole body shuddered with cold. His eyes were stinging with the force of the blowing snow, which was hurting his face.

He heard a bang ahead and jumped. Had that been a gunshot? Or just another tree, cracking in the force of the storm? The wind was so strong he couldn't tell, but knew he had to get inside as fast as he could.

Adrenaline surging, Leblanc slammed open the door of the old cabin, with his gun at the ready. His eyes were swollen and streaming from cold. Dazzled by the white, he could barely see into the gloom.

And then as his vision adjusted, he saw a sight that was worse than he had dreaded. Katie was down, on the floor, clutching at her foot. Behind her, a blonde woman huddled, looking terrified. As she saw him Katie cried out, her voice urgent.

"Katie!" He took a step toward to her, so slow and clumsy with cold that it took him a moment to realize that her cry was not pain. It was a warning. And her eyes were not looking at him, but at something in the corner.

Leblanc tried to turn. He whipped around as fast as he could, but it was too late. Something hit him, hard, on the head. Pain exploded and he reeled back, dazed. his vision blurred and went black. He knew he was going to pass out. His weapon clattered from his numbed hand.

He had to fight, he thought. He had to turn and fight. But instead he dropped to his knees, struggling to look his attacker in the eye.

He'd been hit by the butt of a rifle. The man was turning it now, aiming it. Leblanc, who'd stood up to the worst of hardened criminals, felt his heart thudding with fear.

But at that moment, he realized that Katie was down, but she wasn't out.

Using him as cover, she must have been able to reach her gun while the killer's attention was distracted, because from behind him, he heard a single, quiet word.

"Drop."

Leblanc knew instantly what he had to do. He'd shielded her from the killer's sight and given her the chance she needed. Now, he hit the floor, sprawling down onto the dirty ground, hoping that she would her fire her shot before their attacker could.

The gunshot exploded in his ears. He had no idea whether she'd fired in time, or he had. The only sound was the high-pitched scream of the wind.

Leblanc raised his head. Hc saw the killer was down. Blood was streaming down the side of his head. He couldn't believe that the monster had been taken at last. The man had been haunting his dreams, taunting him with his elusiveness. Now, he was collapsed, unmoving, in the corner of his cabin.

Katie leaped up. Despite her injury, Leblanc was relieved to see she could put weight on her foot. She limped swiftly over to the man, knelt down, and expertly checked him for a pulse.

"Dead," she said briefly.

Behind her, Samantha burst into harsh tears. Leblanc had no idea whether they were from shock, relief, or a combination of the two.

But, with his own head clearing, he knew one thing for sure. They needed to get to safety, and fast, before the storm descended in full fury.

"I'm calling search and rescue. They need to medevac us out of here while they still can," he said, picking up his phone.

CHAPTER THIRTY FOUR

Katie walked slowly into the café on the hospital's ground floor. Her ankle stung painfully, and would for a few more days, but there was no serious damage done. Caleb's first shot had been aimed at her leg and the bullet had only skimmed her. Thanks to Leblanc's arrival, he hadn't shot again.

She was pleased to see Leblanc already in the café, cradling a large cup of hot coffee in his hand. He had a minor head wound and - the doctor had explained to him - had a light concussion.

"You have a very hard head," the doctor had said to him in joking approval as he'd checked him out. In the next-door bed, Katie hadn't been able to suppress a snort of laughter. She agreed with that diagnosis!

Leblanc had given her a look and glanced pointedly at her own head.

She looked at him now, sitting alone, in the quiet of the café. He was staring out of the window at the wilderness beyond, his face serious and thoughtful.

"How's Samantha?" she asked.

"She's been sedated," he said. "She was in shock, and obviously traumatized. Mild exposure. Her husband is with her. She'll be fine."

Katie felt a deep relief that they had been able to save this final victim and put a stop to the killer's spree.

Outside, the snow was battering the windowpanes. The wind was howling. She shivered. Just half an hour later and they would not have been able to go ahead with the rescue operation.

Leblanc looked at Katie. "I still don't understand how you figured it out."

Katie smiled. "It was just a feeling. I realized that something far in his past must have made him who he was, and if we could look back, we might find it. Nothing more than that."

Perhaps her own past, her own family trauma, had been what finally allowed her to join the dots, Katie thought, stirring sugar into her coffee. After all, she knew how events in the distant past could leave lasting scars. For a moment, she wondered if she should go and visit her old home. Her parents didn't even know she was in the area.

She thought about calling them, the way she had so many times in the past. Perhaps now she'd solved this case, it was the time. It was certainly something she should think about.

But no, she decided. She didn't know how they would react, and she wasn't ready to face their anger and accusation again.

Katie realized she was going to miss working with Leblanc. And, in a weird way, she was going to miss the northern elements. Having been in this place from childhood, she'd forgotten how the brutal, dangerous winters made her feel alive. It was a love-hate relationship, she acknowledged.

But it was time to go back to Virginia. Her flight was booked for tomorrow. With the storm forecast to clear later tonight, there was nothing holding her here any longer.

"It's been great working with you. We did well," she said, finishing her coffee and standing up, realizing how much she'd relied on her partner. In the end, they'd worked together seamlessly. They'd saved each other's lives. She felt she understood him now and that she had seen the real man behind the arrogant, opinionated front he portrayed.

"I thought you would insist on taking over. That the investigation would stall, and that it would be smothered by bureaucracy," he explained. "I had the wrong idea about you, at first."

"I guess I did, too," she confessed. "I didn't realize why you were worried, and wondered if you just resented me."

"I did. But I soon changed my mind. Working with you was a privilege. We made a good team," Leblanc said.

He smiled.

*

Two days later, Katie arrived at the FBI head office, at ten a.m. on a crisp, clear winter morning. The sun hung low in a blue sky.

She had been given a few days' leave of absence on her return, to recover from her injury, but Andrews had asked her to come in for a meeting today. She didn't know why. Perhaps he just wanted more information on the case, she thought, heading into the building and taking the stairs to the meeting room on the second floor. She felt refreshed and relaxed, ready to take on whatever Andrews threw at her.

"Good morning, Winter," Andrews said, as she walked into the room.

He was sitting at the large head of a conference table, with his team members on either side. To her surprise, she saw Scott there. What was he doing, she wondered.

"Good morning, gents," Katie said, closing the door behind her and taking a seat near the end of the table.

"I wanted to commend you on how you handled this case," Andrews said, glancing quickly at the team. "It was a huge success. You showed resourcefulness, intuition and courage. We are all very aware how much worse this could have been and how many lives were potentially saved by catching this killer within a couple of days."

For a moment, everyone was silent.

"Thank you," Katie said, still a little puzzled. Why was he talking about the case, when the team had already been debriefed?

"Because this was so successful, and given the number of cross-border crimes that occur in the area, we have decided to make this task force permanent. And you have been invited to join it."

Katie was stunned.

"We challenged you to make a breakthrough on this case quickly, and you did. We want you to stay and help us continue to do this," Scott said. "You have a unique ability to work in this type of environment."

"I do?" Katie asked, still trying to process the news.

"You can handle the conditions. You understand the terrain. You know the background and mentality of the locals in the area. And, over and above all of this, you are able to follow a criminal's thought processes. We solved this case because of you."

Katie felt proud that she'd added such value. But now, this decision was conflicting her seriously.

Move back - permanently - to the place she'd promised never to return?

The place where she'd grown up, and where she'd left behind so much pain and misery. The place where her parents still lived, and where they would be hurt by her very presence, if they even knew.

And yet, how could she turn down this opportunity? One where her specific skillset could be used? Where she'd felt alive? And she had a good relationship with Leblanc. After a rocky start he had proven to be a brilliant case partner, and he'd had her back. Saved her life.

"How long do I have to decide?" Katie said, at last.

"I know it's a big decision," Andrews said. "You have till the end of the week. When you come back from leave on Monday, I'll need your decision by then."

"Thank you," Katie said.

She had time to decide, time to think about it.

But, as she left the meeting room, she realized she already knew what her answer would be.

NOW AVAILABLE!

<u>REACH ME</u>
(A Katie Winter FBI Suspense Thriller —Book 2)

When a serial killer escapes and crosses the border into Canada, FBI Special Agent Katie Winter must team up with her Canadian counterpart to stop him before others die. But as secrets from her own past bubble up, Katie must also follow a lead for her own sister's disappearance before it, too, goes cold.

"Molly Black has written a taut thriller that will keep you on the edge of your seat… I absolutely loved this book and can't wait to read the next book in the series!"
—Reader review for Girl One: Murder

REACH ME is book #2 in a new series by #1 bestselling mystery and suspense author Molly Black.

FBI Special Agent Katie Winter is no stranger to frigid winters, isolation, and dangerous cases. With her sterling record of hunting down serial killers, she is a fast-rising star in the BAU, and Katie is the natural choice to partner with Canadian law enforcement to track the killer across the brutal and unforgiving landscape.

Yet Katie's past haunts her, demanding her attention and dragging her down into a well of secrets. Will this killer take advantage of Katie's weakness?

Can she stop him in time?

Or will he find her first?

A complex psychological crime thriller full of twists and turns and packed with heart-pounding suspense, the KATIE WINTER mystery series will make you fall in love with a brilliant new female protagonist and keep you turning pages late into the night.

Book #3 in the series—HIDE ME—is now also available.

Molly Black

Debut author Molly Black is author of the MAYA GRAY FBI suspense thriller series, comprising six books (and counting); the RYLIE WOLF FBI suspense thriller series, comprising three books (and counting); of the TAYLOR SAGE FBI suspense thriller series, comprising three books (and counting); and of the KATIE WINTER FBI suspense thriller series, comprising three books (and counting).

An avid reader and lifelong fan of the mystery and thriller genres, Molly loves to hear from you, so please feel free to visit www.mollyblackauthor.com to learn more and stay in touch.

BOOKS BY MOLLY BLACK

MAYA GRAY MYSTERY SERIES
GIRL ONE: MURDER (Book #1)
GIRL TWO: TAKEN (Book #2)
GIRL THREE: TRAPPED (Book #3)
GIRL FOUR: LURED (Book #4)
GIRL FIVE: BOUND (Book #5)
GIRL SIX: FORSAKEN (Book #6)

RYLIE WOLF FBI SUSPENSE THRILLER
FOUND YOU (Book #1)
CAUGHT YOU (Book #2)
SEE YOU (Book #3)

TAYLOR SAGE FBI SUSPENSE THRILLER
DON'T LOOK (Book #1)
DON'T BREATHE (Book #2)
DON'T RUN (Book #3)

KATIE WINTER FBI SUSPENSE THRILLER
SAVE ME (Book #1)
REACH ME (Book #2)
HIDE ME (Book #3)

Made in the USA
Columbia, SC
03 April 2022